HIGhWAY 28 WEST

❦

JOE TAYLOR

Sagging Meniscus

© 2023 by Joe Taylor

All Rights Reserved.

Set in Sabon with LaTeX.

ISBN: 978-1-952386-60-2 (paperback)
ISBN: 978-1-952386-61-9 (ebook)
Library of Congress Control Number: 2023935878

Sagging Meniscus Press
Montclair, New Jersey
saggingmeniscus.com

Appreciation goes to the Sumter Scribblers for their help on this book. Tricia Taylor, Christin Loehr and in memory of Sarah Langcuster, much missed.

Contents

New York Minute   1

Pup   27

Sea Change, or, The Truth   46

Math Speaks: *Go. Scatter.*   81

Yellow Fever   97

Highway 28 West

New York Minute

PREACHER: (*Scrambling onto a picnic table to stare at a gathering crowd until reluctantly speaking.*)

I think I should warn all of you before I begin: at the end of my tale, no one is left standing, all have fallen, all are dead.

(*A tidal wave of laughter slaps PREACHER's face. It continues for an uncomfortable time. PREACHER shifts on his feet, uncertain. He looks about, then under the table, calls out something quietly, licks his lips, sticks his right hand in his right pocket, and retrieves . . . nothing. As if realizing where he is, speaks again.*)

PREACHER:

Why . . . why are you all laughing? It's . . . it's sad. It's tragic. *All* will fall. All. Why are you laughing?

SELF-APPOINTED SPOKESMAN: (*This man pushes forward. He stands stiff and tall, his eyes have sunken backwards into his face, pulling skin in with them, leaving what passes for a patina of bone. An onlooker could not discern the color of his eyes, only that they are abnormally with-*

drawn. Likewise, his hair is thinning and patchy. It may be sandy, it may be salt and pepper.)

There's no difference, Preacher, in your tale than any other we've ever heard. That's why we're laughing. Do you think we're children to be warned and coddled? (*A baby cries out, to be hushed by its mother, who pops her hand over its mouth in a rhythm, leaving a* waa-waa *sound echoing in the open air, as if the firmament were eternally, perhaps empathetically, perhaps mockingly, perhaps unknowingly, rebounding that* waa-waa *back to the abiding earth.*) You see what I mean, Preacher? Even that baby knows. Tears is all there ever is, in the end. Weeping and tears. But you go on with your tale. We need us some distraction.

WOMAN IN CROWD:

Go on! Tell us your tale!

. . . Highway 28 West, if you were driving along it, would seem to stretch out like the far-reaching arm of a god unfurling, with fingers twitching to entice you onward at the top of a rise, to just the point where a stand of pines off a mile distant disappears in a swirl of emerald pollen. *Ah! Fall*, you might think, gripping the steering wheel. And you would not be wrong. Nor would you be right, for just beyond those pines lies a sharp curve (which has taken eleven lives in the last six decades), and beyond that curve a vicious snowstorm swirls, well into its second hour. Three inches have accumulated, and Highway 28 West is already treacherous. By nightfall it will become impassable. But do not mistake this for barren, dying winter—no, for spring traipses ahead! Yes, spring jostles just beyond that cluster of three mobile homes, beyond that one frozen small pond, which fingers itself near the highway, beyond that dead cardinal whose hungry mouth opens to nothing, beyond that smattering of deer, opossum, rats, and beetles scavenging for food.

The riot of spring, glorious and imperious spring! Its emeralds, its pinks, its reds! A snake slithers across the warming blacktop of the highway, a shower rains down on The Eternal Truth of Jesus Christ on Calvary Church, which was built as close to Highway 28 West as laws would allow some fifty-nine years ago, so that Jesus the Christ might perch in imminent numerical judgment. Clouds overhead grow denser and darker, and the happy buds of the eleven sweet gum trees rooted beside the church flutter, anxious in the wind. The original minister's wife had planted flowering pink dogwoods, but these sweet gums invaded and took over, long before the minister and his wife lay on their deathbeds. Now, their graves look forward to soaking up whatever rain they can, while the sweet gums tremble from gusts of cold wind that threaten harsher weather, even a small twister. Driving on seems advisable.

So. Another curve, and then another. The temperature rises noticeably. Three vultures are tugging at a dead armadillo, worrying its shell to get at the swelling flesh. To avoid them, a slight swerve to the left becomes necessary—a careful swerve so as to not collide with the eighteen-wheeler pulling a load of pine that probably would be ticketed as overweight and unsafe, if any state trooper ever were to pass by. But there's not enough money to provide that service. There may never be. If you have a wreck, pick a favorite god and pray.

It's a scorcher on this part of the highway, this late-morning. The sun has made a bet with the moon that it can top 100 degrees by two p.m. Neither sun nor moon comment on global warming; though they do rotate and revolve happily since the invention of thermometers, which provide a goal in an otherwise boring cycle of rotating, rising, setting. Another, more earnest bet between the two . . . well, the time for revealing that bet awaits. But there *is* a second bet betwixt them. Earth and the other planets, comets, asteroids, and stars, aren't particularly welcome to participate in these wagers, and never have been, for the sun and moon make a cozy, private couple. It's 11 a.m. It's ninety-three degrees. It seems as if the sun will easily win the first bet.

SELF-APPOINTED SPOKESMAN:

Hey, Preacher! Get on with your tale. We're waiting with bated death rattles. (*Scattered laughter.*)

PREACHER:

I'm not really a preacher, you know. It's just a nickname I got in high school. (*'Do tell,' a woman in the crowd shouts. 'Yeah, do tell,' a man counters. 'Just do tell us something,' another woman shouts, ' 'cause it's boring out here.'*)

PREACHER:

It was winter. It was snowing hard. My pick-up had stalled half a mile back, so I left it on the side of the road. I spotted two trailers ahead. There was a small pond, all frozen over, reaching out toward the highway, like it was ready to expand and encase the road in a more serious, more dangerous ice. The nearest trailer was the largest, a doublewide. A triplewide. Do they even make those? Whatever, it actually had a metal chimney with smoke coming out. It offered warmth and some help maybe.

VOICE OF TEENAGE BOY FROM CROWD:

Why didn't you just use your cellphone?!

PREACHER:

Warmth and help, maybe. So I headed toward it. A dog from another of the trailers barked, but someone yelled it to *Hush*! A dead cardinal lay in the yard in front of me. This had been a tough winter, and it was only beginning. I paused to look at the bird, a bright red male. Its claws curled as if grasping one last branch. Its eyes were gone, leaving a crust. Its beak opened hungrily for the nothing. I stepped over it. Shouting was coming from the doublewide, triplewide mobile home. Angry. A woman and a man, the eternal struggle. I guess it could have been a man and man, or a woman and a woman, and I would be obliged to say the same. The eternal struggle. Two children even, toddlers. Shouting. Grabbing. Hitting. The eternal struggle. I wondered where the cardinal's mate had gone. I came close enough to see the large, fancy window bulging out from the trailer. I shuddered, for a shotgun hung over the mantel of the friendly fireplace inside. I remembered a sad rule about mantels and guns.

TEENAGE BOY FROM CROWD:

Just shoot the damn thing!

WOMAN IN CROWD:

I don't like hunters. Their blood's too hot.

PREACHER:

I could see the woman now. Her finger was wagging at the man. Her face was contorted and red. Her mouth made a large zero, large enough to match her wild eyes. She was wearing a royal blue bathrobe. I stepped up onto the large deck out front. A snow-covered barbecue grill leaned against the trailer. One of its legs was rusted out and broken. The cardinal's mate flew out from it with that first vibrating step of mine. The two inside turned to look at me when I took my second step. I shivered and waved uncertainly, like a shy, anorexic high school beauty contestant sitting in a convertible and fated to finish dead last. Who had entered her against her will? Who had painted her up so? Frozen her hair so wild and silly? Pushed her young breasts up so gaudy? Why the futility? Why? Why? The man inside the trailer yanked himself about—so it seemed from my viewpoint, anyhow. I mean that he was moving quickly and jerkily toward the door, as if pushed and then pulled by an amused puppeteer.

CECIL: (*Yanking trailer door open.*)

What the hell you selling?!

SHERRY:

Cecil, you idiot! He's not a salesman in this weather! He must be in trouble. Let him in out of the snow.

. . . The snow, as if to prove Cecil right and Sherry wrong, abruptly stopped. The dog from the other, off-ways trailer barked again, to be hit and then whimper sharply. The fire in this one's fireplace, under the mantel holding the shotgun, popped an ember out against the screen. A pile of dirty clothes that would all and each gladly welcome any glowing ember and happily catch fire sulked, disappointed that the screen had interfered with their plans. The man named Preacher stomped his left foot, then his right. Then he shivered in agreement with the woman, and said,

PREACHER:

If you don't mind, my truck stalled out down the highway. I'd like to use a phone.

CECIL:

You don't got no cell phone?

SHERRY:

Let him in, you jerk. The cold is blowing hard.

PREACHER:

Obliged, ma'am.

CECIL:

I recognize you! You're the one they call Preacher.

PREACHER:

They just call me that. I'm not really one. I guess I really don't know what I believe.

CECIL:

Well that's dumb as hell, you ask me.

SHERRY:

No one asked you, Cecil! Be polite. Let the man use your cell phone and call some help.

CECIL:

How come you don't let him use your'n?

SHERRY:

Asshole!

. . . The woman pushes back a curl looping over her left eye, gives Preacher a smile, and searches in a large multi-colored purse sitting atop a table. Preacher can see a golden giraffe on the purse, a red lion, a purple monkey. Retrieving a pink cell phone after jangling keys and misfiring a spray can of some unidentified content that fills the air and makes Preacher sneeze, she winks and hands the pink cell phone to Preacher. She brushes his fingers with her long, long nails that are polished deep purple. 'Obliged,' Preacher says. 'Damn right,' Cecil comments. Preacher ignores him to make a call. He's told that a tow truck can't come for at least three hours, sometime mid-afternoon. Preacher looks at the fire, at the woman, and then at Cecil.

CECIL:

You can't stay here. We're having a discussion.

SHERRY:

We're having a screaming, drag-down argument, is what we're having, you idiot.

CECIL:

So he can't stay here.

SHERRY:

It's my 'manufactured home' too. I say he can. I'll make some coffee. I like his looks. (*She pauses and frowns at Cecil.*) A lot better than I like yours.

PREACHER:

If it's no bother . . . it is cold out there.

CECIL:

It is a bother.

SHERRY:

It's not. Shut up, Cecil. Go play on your short wave—

CECIL:

It's a ham radio!

SHERRY:

Go play on your pork chop radio and talk to your nutcase survivalist idiot friends. Locate a cave to hide out in for when the darkies and the liberals take over the government and come hunting down idiots. There's some big deep caverns sixty miles north of here.

CECIL:

Sometimes, woman . . .

VOICE FROM CROWD:

We can stream better than this on Netflix or Hulu.

ANOTHER VOICE:

That's if the Internet's up and working.

TEENAGE BOY:

Just shoot the damn gun!

WOMAN IN CROWD:

Hunters is mean. They kill things just for sport. I don't like cats neither.

LIZZIE, GIRL POET IN CROWD:

The people, they chant,
The people, they sing.
They jostle, they rant,
They don't mean a thing.

PREACHER: (*Inhaling deeply.*)

Once upon a time, there was this man and this woman. They met in a small town bar with lions and zebras painted on the walls, or in a sweaty tent revival filled with pictures of longhaired glowing Jesuses, or in an air-conditioned post office filled with mug shots of hard-eyed criminals.

The man had a good job as a supervisor at a boxing company plant, the woman worked the purchasing department of the local college. The man was handsome, with curly black hair like maybe a rock or movie star—Jack White or a young John Travolta. The woman was beautiful, stately with blonde hair like maybe Lady Gaga. They fell deep in lust and married and bought a piece of land with a pond and a new manufactured home with bay windows jutting out just like it was something real from England. It even had a fireplace and a chimney.

Well, the woman was just too damn good looking. She started kit-catting around at the college. The man began drinking. They became unhappy. The man bought a shotgun and racked it over the fireplace, thinking to assert his authority. He'd only hunted once in his life, and that time he'd fallen in a ditch and busted up his ankle. Stop me, if you've heard this before . . .

ANOTHER WOMAN IN CROWD:

He's talking about my second cousin.

MAN IN CROWD:

Naw, he's talking about that high-toned blonde woman moved here from the city five years ago, the one they said killed her husband and her self.

WOMAN IN CROWD:

Some people claim a burglar broke in. There was a man seen around.

PREACHER:

This woman, she had gone hunting lots of times because she was the only child of a man who wanted a son. She killed an eight-point buck when she was twelve and she got her face smeared with its blood. She remembered how warm the blood felt on her cheeks and how it tingled down to her fundament.

So like I said, this man began drinking.

WOMAN IN CROWD:

Don't they always?

SECOND WOMAN:

Amen, sister.

SELF-APPOINTED SPOKESMAN IN CROWD:

Hush, let him tell his tale.

PREACHER:

Then one cold snowy morning when they were arguing about the man's drinking—he'd shown up to work at the box plant drunk and been sent home with a warning—so then one cold snowy morning, this man shows up at their door, saying his truck was stuck down the road, and asking if he could use their phone to call a wrecker. The woman, she'd seen this man before and liked his looks. She made him some coffee and loaned him her cell phone. Her husband sneaked into the bathroom to get a shot of whiskey and steady his shakes. The man who'd showed up at the door learned over the cell phone that the wrecker couldn't come for at least three hours. The woman heard her husband opening the little drawer in the bathroom where he kept his whiskey hid. She eased up to the man holding the pink cell phone and took it from his hand and gave him a cup of coffee, rubbing her hip against him and brushing her cheek with the warm coffee cup, which reminded her of something, she couldn't remember what, but it stirred her down to her fundament. In the bathroom, her husband coughed. He opened the little drawer again. She could almost hear him gulping down the whiskey. 'Let's go sit on the divan,' the woman said to the man with the coffee mug. 'Divan,' was what word she said, but it came out in long, tall syllables that sounded more like 'divine.'

So they sat on the couch, the woman easing closer as the man drank his coffee and warmed his hands on the mug and looked at the fire. 'Would you kindly put another log on the fire,' the woman asked. She stretched out the word 'fire,' so maybe it sounded like three or four words that the man wasn't sure about. He got up and put a log on the fire. And then another. The husband was still in the bathroom. He turned on a country station in there, loud. In the song, someone was drinking and missing his woman.

'How would you like to scootch on over here and really get warm?' the woman asked the man who stood by the fire. She patted the divan. Her pats all seemed to be three or four words long. And then she rubbed the divan with her hands and their long purple nails. Her blue bathrobe was parted, and the man thought he saw a dark, dark nipple. Its peeping out reminded him of something, maybe a childhood game. 'Don't you worry. He's in there drinking, staring at the tiles on the floor. He'll stay there till he passes out. He never looks in the mirror, he never comes out. He *wants* us to do it, so he don't have to. A woman has needs. At least three hours. I heard what that man said on the phone.'

The man looked from the fireplace to the nipple to the woman to the bathroom. 'It's cold outside,' was all he said. Then he walked over and sat down.

Twenty-two minutes later, the woman grabbed her robe and put it back on. She stared at the man who'd come to her door. Her eyes seemed to get tighter and tighter, like some kind of vise. 'There ain't no real men these days,' she said finally. 'Why don't you just get on out of here. You got what you came for. Put another log on the fire before you go. I've had it. I'm going to take that shotgun down and kill that drunken son of a bitch while he's sober enough to know I'm doing it, while he sits on the toilet bowl shaking and slobbering. So you get on out of here, before I decide to kill you too.'

The man looked in her eyes. They were a blue that might match her bathrobe except they were so mad and so tight. He eyed the shotgun stretching over the mantel and stood to pull on his trousers and shirt and coat. 'Log. Don't forget the log.' He glanced at the woman's feet, which had long purple nails too. On one foot, she wore a silver toe ring on her toe next to her big toe. All her toes curled and gripped the gold-brown carpet in the mobile home like she needed balance even though she was sitting. He passed the shotgun on the mantel and lifted a log from the stack, tossing it on the fire. 'Git,' the woman hissed. She stood and looked at the shotgun.

He opened the door and left. He heard the woman hiss, 'Git!' again behind the thin trailer door as it shut. After stepping over the dead cardinal, he started to run. As he ran past the first trailer he heard a blast coming from the trailer he'd left. The dog began to bark. Someone screamed and hit it. The dog yelped and stopped. The man was nearing the second trailer. He ran on. There was a third trailer ahead. He hadn't seen it before, but he could see it now. It had been hidden, maybe since it was past the frozen pond, which he skirted, afraid that he'd either slip on the ice or that the ice was too thin and would break and he'd fall in. When he skirted the pond and started up a small rise for the last trailer that had been hidden, he heard a second blast. He stopped and looked back. The trailer he'd been in back there looked the same through the snow and the barren trees. He knew it wasn't, though.

BOY IN THE CROWD:

About time someone shot that gun off.

LIZZIE, GIRL POET IN CROWD:

The stars, they twinkle,
And wishes get made.
Some get granted,
Some get the blade.

... The snow started up again, slowly at first, as if a dancer initiating warm-ups before a big city ballet. Where do birds go when it snows, the man wondered. He remembered the female cardinal hiding in the leaning, rusty, three-legged grill. She likely wasn't there now. There was only snow and him and wind. He might as well have been on an outer, cold planet, not even of this solar system, but some far-off, lost other, one that would never talk with the sun and the moon. He stopped. He didn't want to look back at that first trailer, but he did, expecting maybe it would be aflame from a knocked over fireplace screen and that pile of clothes. But it wasn't. It looked the same. But it wasn't.

ANNA:

I heard two shotgun blasts. I've been watching you through the window. My neighbor called, said the shots came from the fancy doublewide Burrell trailer. I wouldn't be at all surprised if they killed one another. My neighbor said a man ran from the trailer after being in there for near an hour. (*She pauses to look at the man before her, leaning expectantly as if he might be an angelic messenger.*) Would that be you?

PREACHER:

It was me, all right. That woman in the doublewide—Sherry?—she said she was going to kill her husband and she threatened she might kill me. That's why I ran this way toward your trailer. My truck, it's back half a mile or more that other way.

ANNA: (*Nodding and wringing her hands.*)

That sounds right. They been fighting for two years. My husband works—worked, cause he's taken awful sick for three weeks—with the man Cecil Burrell. My husband says Cecil comes in drunk all the time. I heard they caught him a week ago and maybe laid him off. My neighbor who called is her second cousin, Sherry's cousin, that is. They went to the college in town together. My neighbor said she heard a scream and then the shotgun. And then, about the time I saw you, the second shotgun came. My neighbor said they'd been screaming most of the morning. She called the sheriff. He said he won't be able to come for at least two hours.

. . . The man named Preacher let out a bitter laugh. 'What's so funny?' the woman named Anna asked him. 'That's the same thing the wrecker people told me an hour ago. They said they couldn't be here for three hours then. Two hours now.' The woman named Anna considered, swaying in the doorway. 'That's the way it is on this highway. Everything takes at least two hours or two days or two months or two years longer than it should.' There was a syrupy, prolonged cough behind her, from within the trailer. 'Unless it's something bad, and then it happens a lot quicker than it should, in a "New York minute," like a friend of mine used to say.'

She looked at the man named Preacher. He looked at her. She was wringing her hands, which were raw and red. Her head was half-cocked backward, listening for something within the trailer.

ANNA:

I'd ask you in from the cold, but like I said, my husband and my boy have taken bad sick. I don't know why I haven't caught whatever it is. I can give you some coffee, though, to keep you warm while you wait for that tow truck. *(She pauses, looking into Preacher's eyes.)* You know, the weirdest thing, I thought when I peeped at you running up that little rise—don't laugh—but I thought maybe you were a messenger angel from God, come to save my boy and my husband. They're awful sick.

PREACHER:

I wish I were. I do indeed wish I were. They seen a doctor?

ANNA:

My husband don't believe in doctors and hospitals and such. My boy's teacher at school says she might have to report us to Welfare if we don't get the boy to a doctor. *(She wrings her hands, which are cracked and ready to bleed.)* Let me get you that big mug of coffee. I just brewed it. The highway's right down there, if you cut toward those three oaks.

PREACHER:

I'm obliged.

. . . The snow has thickened. Preacher walks toward the three oak trees. Behind, there's no sound other than an occasional falling branch, burdened with snow. He reaches the highway, which now has a good four inches of snow on it. He wonders how many ninety-six-cent tubs of Morton forever-flow salt it would take to clear a path back to his truck. Five thousand? Ten thousand? Part of him wants to sit down with the big mug of coffee—its blue matches the woman named Sherry's robe and her eyes—wants to sit down on the highway and just . . . just what, he wonders. He holds the coffee mug to his cheek.

An hour and a half later, the tow truck shows.

GENE'S TOWING SERVICE:

Got here a bit early. Good thing, because this highway's about had it for travel, you know?

PREACHER:

Yes, I was thinking the same.

GENE'S TOWING SERVICE:

Any idea what's wrong?

PREACHER:

I hit a bump and it just stopped.

... The driver is tall. He's six-foot-six, if an inch. He must weigh nearly 300 pounds, most of it gnarly muscle. Preacher wonders, *What if he was the one to visit the woman named Sherry? Would he have been man enough?* And then Preacher wonders, *What if he had visited that woman and her dying husband and son? Would he have cured them like an angel?*

'Mind if I look under the hood?' the huge man asks. Preacher says 'Certainly not.' So Preacher gets in the truck and pops the hood and the man tinkers around, goes to his tow truck and comes back with a screwdriver and a socket wrench. He knocks the wrench against the engine of Preacher's truck. It gives a quick metallic *Clonk!* He's bent over under the hood, and in his dark green work suit he looks like a swamp tree weighted with slowly swaying moss. 'Battery'd jiggled loose,' the man says finally, emerging from under the hood. 'I'll just charge you what I would have to tow you in to Hank's gas station.' The man turns to look off at the highway a bit.

GENE'S TOWING SERVICE:

You know there was a murder up there of last spring. Woman killed her husband, then herself, though some say a stranger'd come by and did it, because there weren't no suicide note. Folks say the house is haunted. It's a two-story, fancy deal. You'd think some hotshot professor from the college in town would buy it up. But the dead woman worked there, at the college. They say it's haunted. People is funny about that type of thing. They say you can hear them screaming at one another of nighttime, that their screams follow along under the leaves of all the trees.—No, I can't take American Express. Yep, that MasterCard will work . . .

LIZZIE, GIRL POET IN CROWD:

There are those who know,
And those who think they know.
Say what's the diff?
A coffin's lid will close the show.

WOMAN IN CROWD:

Can't you shut her up? She's your daughter.

MOTHER IN CROWD:

Her father says she's a 'prodigy,' says she has 'poetic genius.'

WOMAN IN CROWD:

Well, I just wish she'd shut up. I can't stand it.

PREACHER:

The man named Preacher drove his pickup on into town. He made it to a hamburger place just before they closed, where he bought a burger and some onion rings. He decided that he'd better spend the night in his truck, rather than risking driving along the highway to his home.

VOICE IN CROWD:

Don't lie to us, Preacher! You don't got no home!

PREACHER:

I do. It's a little three-room brick house just north of here. (*He points.*)

MAN IN CROWD:

That's west, not north. Go on and admit it, Preacher, you ain't got no home but that black pick-up.

. . . Preacher fell asleep, wishing he had at least a dog to keep him warm. He didn't have enough gasoline to run the truck and its heater all night. He must have dreamed. Everyone dreams, but Preacher couldn't remember a thing when the sun woke him. He never could. There was a little bit of coffee left from the woman named Anna. It was cold, but he drank it anyways. Just before noon, the sun had melted most of the snow on the streets. Preacher noticed folk driving in couples, all dressed in black, all heading out Highway 28 West. There were kids in some of the cars, and they were dressed in black, too. After the twentieth or so car, he decided to follow one with an old woman and old man, the woman driving, bent over the steering wheel and concentrating, with the man staring forward, ready to warn her of any up-ahead danger.

He followed them past the spot where his truck had stalled. He saw that the wrecker man had dropped a green kerchief on the side of the road. He followed them past the three trailers. Ahead of them, other cars and trucks were all and each pulling into the dirt and gravel parking lot behind The Eternal Truth of Jesus Christ on Calvary Church. Which is where he followed the car with the old couple. There must have been fifty, sixty cars and trucks already parked there. Preacher got out after the couple he'd followed got out and lurched toward the church's door. He heard gravel crunch under their uneven, wobbling steps. He could see now that they were in their seventies, even eighties. They hobbled up the two steps, where a man dressed in oily black stood. This man didn't acknowledge the couple, and they didn't acknowledge him. When Preacher walked by, he tried to see the man's eyes, even his lips or his face, but the man turned from him. 'Warmed up, hasn't it? Snow'll all be gone by tomorrow,' Preacher said. The man didn't respond.

Preacher walked into the church. Where'd they get all those flowers in the middle of this nasty winter, he wondered. Mexico? Past all the drug cartels? The front of the church was filled, three tiers high, with roses and lilies and other flowers Preacher couldn't even guess at. Purple, pink, yellow, white. He sneezed. Five people in the last row turned around and frowned at him, as if the intrusive, vulgar noise were his fault. Preacher shrugged. There were two caskets up front, and folks were marching by them. A woman stood wringing her hands. She stood between the two caskets, which were open for inspection, like maybe she wanted to prove she didn't strangle or shoot or chop the two dead people. Preacher's eyes widened. It was the same woman who'd given him the big blue mug of coffee just so soon ago. People were clasping her right hand, pulling it from the comfort and busyness of wringing her left hand. They were pumping her right hand like it was connected to a deep, crystal freshwater well. Preacher got in the line to march up and view the bodies. The line moved like an uncertain spider tumbling over rotting leaves, with starts and stops. He got close enough that he could see a man with an unruly salt and pepper beard propped in one casket, a boy of thirteen or so with an abnormally long face in the other. Preacher inched closer. The woman's face didn't look like it did yesterday when she thought he might be an angel come to save her husband and boy. It didn't look at all. It just jiggled when people pumped her right hand extra hard. Her hair bounced along with her face.

Preacher sat down in a pew. There was no reason to prolong her standing there, bouncing and jiggling and pumping. He closed his eyes and thought of what she said about the highway. Things you want always take hours and days and months and years. Things like death shoot straight at you in a New York minute. Like this funeral and the two caskets. Preacher kept his eyes shut tight while a granky organ sounded.

WOMAN IN CROWD:

So. You there, girl. You got any smartass poem for that?

LIZZIE, THE GIRL POET: (*Stands with her arms folded before her. She doesn't respond. The woman starts for her, to shake her, but is stopped.*)

MOTHER IN CROWD:

Leave Lizzie alone. She went to school with that boy.

. . . Too much snow, too many funerals. The preacher man in his suit and tie told them that God had a plan for the young boy and his father. They all stared mutely as his words drifted in and out of their ears, as they swam over and through their haircuts and hairdos, over the perfumed stink of the flowers. It wasn't a very good one, Preacher thought, the plan this so-called God had, that is. Maybe a fresh new blueprint would help. A woman to his right turned and scowled as if she'd read his mind.

Pup

. . . Preacher left The Eternal Truth of Jesus Christ on Calvary Church, not even knowing which way he turned onto the highway. He was backtracking, he realized after passing that third trailer, then *pop, pop, pop*, coming on the other two. Backtracking can be good, he thought. He rolled down his window, despite the chill. He heard his tires throwing slush and water from the highway. Backtracking can be like dreaming, he thought. A filing system to store some things close by, push others into the attic or even a far-off storage shed. Was that why he could never remember his dreams, then? Was every dream of his lugged away to be tossed into some off-site rental storage shed? Was that where they all went? Was it even climate-controlled? And he didn't have the money to pay the rental, so he'd never get to visit and talk with them, to learn just what it was they were filing away.

He'd have to find work, and soon. The boxing plant. They'd need help now.

Ahead, there lay the green bandana. Preacher pulled over to the shoulder of the road. He looked in his side mirror back along the highway. He thought he could see the start of the funeral procession, its headlights beaming at him in judgment. *You weren't the one to die. You weren't the one to die. Why? Why?* He crossed the road and picked up the green bandana. He heard a shuffling and a whimper. A pit bull puppy sat up above him on a gouged-out rise beside an oak tree, wagging its tail unsurely.

WOMAN IN CROWD:

You're the one stole my son's puppy! He cried for a week!

MAN IN CROWD:

Jane, there must be ten thousand pit bulls at any given time in these five counties. Two thousand a county.

WOMAN IN CROWD:

He's the one! I can see it in his eyes!

. . . Preacher looked up at the puppy. 'You a girl or a boy?' he asked it. The puppy wagged its tail at Preacher's tone. 'That's all right. It doesn't matter. You're in for the haul one way or another.' Preacher scrambled up the side of the hillock, pulling himself by an exposed root. The puppy yipped once and then rolled over. She was a she. Beside her lay the tawny feathers of a female cardinal. Preacher gave the pup a pat on its pink, scratched-up tummy and gathered the feathers in his hand. 'And you, old gal, are out of it now. No more hiding in a rusty grill, no more wondering where your mate flew off to.' Preacher pulled out his pocketknife to dig a little grave, which the puppy worried at until Preacher gave it the green bandana. 'Got something better in the car for you, Pup. Leftover sausage and biscuit. That suit you?'

But they couldn't cross the road since the funeral procession came upon them, heading for the cemetery in town. Two black hearses. Which one did she ride in, her boy's or her husband's? Did she blame her husband and his distrust of doctors for her boy's death? Did the minister and the funeral director with their fine suits and ties just lead her willy-nilly to one of the limousines and ease her in, unawares?

The headlights glared at Preacher and now at Pup. *You weren't the ones to die. You weren't the ones to die. Why? Why?*

LIZZIE, GIRL POET IN CROWD

Bones in your coffee,
Blood in your wine.
Drink 'em up fast,
You don't got much time.

PREACHER:

I took Pup with me when I applied for that job at the boxing plant. Pup was good luck, 'cause I got the job right away. 'Graveyard shift's all we got,' the boss guy said. 'That suits me to a tee,' I answered.

WOMAN IN CROWD:

Sure beginning to sound that way.

MAN IN CROWD:

Let him tell his tale.

. . . Eight days later, Pup and Preacher were riding the highway. He'd cashed his first paycheck. He and Pup were eating fried chicken and green beans and biscuits. Pup popped up on the dashboard and growled. There was an old Black man ahead, just sitting on the side of the highway, his head hung down. Preacher pulled over and yelled back.

PREACHER:

You okay? You need some help?

OLD MAN:

I's fine. Just tired, dog-tired.

PREACHER:

I can give you a lift somewhere. Me and Pup are only out driving around, so I can take you back to the town or wherever.

OLD MAN: (*Looking up, a small smile.*)

I's afraid of dogs.

PREACHER:

You can ride in the bed of the truck then. I can pass you a chicken leg through the back window. Just bought it, still hot.

OLD MAN: (*Getting up with a struggle.*)

I like me some fried chicken. My wife and two sons and grandkids, they all back thataway, two mile.

PREACHER:

Hush up, Pup. Come on, then. I'll drive you there. Here, you sure you won't just get in the cab? Pup's just a puppy. He loves everybody.

OLD MAN:

He be like Jesus then? Love ever'body?

. . . Preacher wasn't sure how to respond. He remembered the minister and God's lousy plan. He remembered a railroad track and a bent metal switching box. He remembered too much. Too much. Where was the storage shed when he needed it? A breeze blew by them both, and Preacher could now smell the old man, who stunk like sopping urine. Preacher thought maybe it'd be just as well he rode along in the bed of the truck. 'Here, let me help you climb up. Just sit on the tailgate and then we can scoot you along toward the cab.' 'That pup got pit-bull eyes. You sure he don't bite?' 'I'm sure. All she does is slobber and paw and love on folk.' 'Like Jesus then?' the old man said again. 'Like Jesus,' Preacher replied this time, thinking at least the slobbering and pawing part had to be right.

The old man scooted himself along the black bed of Preacher's truck and said, 'One-a my son went ta that college in town. Got him a degree and got a good job in the city. Other got him a government loan and opened him a little helpin' place for old folk like me and my wife. Carry them about to doctors and bank and grocery sto' and such. He a loving fellow.' 'Like Jesus,' Preacher commented, giving a blink. 'Yes, like Jesus,' the old man replied.

PREACHER:

Folks, I hate to tell you this, but I have to. All that was a lie. A terrible tall-tale lie just to make you and me feel good for a passing moment or so. That old man had died sometime in the night, and he had sat there slumped beside the highway. People'd just driven on by, maybe blowing their horns as a joke to wake him up, I don't know. But he was stiff when I walked up to him, so I did know he'd been dead some time. The ambulance came when I called them on my new cell phone. I waited for them to show there. Me and Pup talked to the old man while we waited. He didn't answer, so me and Pup figured he was awfully smart.

AMBULANCE WOMAN:

Lord God, it's RaeJon's daddy.

AMBULANCE MAN: (*Holding two fingers to the old man's neck, pulling away quickly.*)

He's dead, all right. I'll go call the cops.

AMBULANCE WOMAN: (*To Preacher and Pup, whom she smiles at.*)

Gotta call them if it's suspicious, like no doctor around. On the side of the road.

PREACHER:

You find many along the side of a road?

AMBULANCE WOMAN:

On *this* highway? You bet. All the time. The Highway To Hell, I call it. This isn't a happy highway. Your pup's cute. What's its name?

PREACHER:

Pup. I found her just last week. I thought about naming her New York Minute, but it's too long.

AMBULANCE WOMAN:

You could just call her 'New York.' Or maybe 'Minute.' Why'd you want to name her that?

PREACHER:

Because she changed my luck. I got a job.

AMBULANCE WOMAN:

Well that's good. Pets are good for folk, helps 'em smile.

AMBULANCE MAN:

Sheriff's coming right away.

AMBULANCE WOMAN:

In a New York minute?

. . . So Preacher, Pup, the old dead man who won't answer any questions, and the two ambulance drivers stand and wait. Within a New York Minute, the highway is littered with cars, trucks, and people. Two sheriff cars from the county have arrived. Two patrol cars from town have arrived, even though this part of the highway is out of their jurisdiction. They're curious and have nothing else to do. Gene's Towing Service has arrived, since he misunderstood the cop-wave band and thought there was a wreck. The old man's son, RaeJon, will soon arrive. Two passers-by have stopped. One bored town cop is standing directing traffic, the other stands staring from Preacher to the dead man. 'You're the one who found him?' asks a sheriff's deputy, a thin Black man. 'That's right,' replies Preacher. 'I was driving by and thought maybe he was sick and needed help.' 'Ain't you the one they call Preacher, the one who found that dead girl on the railroad tracks up about three miles ahead?' the cop from town who's been staring asks. 'Yes, that's me.' 'Bad luck seems to sorter follow you around, don't it?' 'Not anymore,' Preacher replies. 'Not since Pup here. He's changed my luck.' 'Ain't *your* luck needs changin', but the people you meet,' the town cop insists. 'My luck changed for the worse, since I lost my best green bandana,' Gene's Towing Service says, wiping his brow with another, lighter green bandana. Preacher holds Pup closer to his side. 'Well what's that one you got there?' the town cop who's not directing traffic asks Gene. 'Not the same. Feels different, smells different. Here, wanna smell?' The town cop who's not directing traffic backs away and everyone laughs.

PREACHER:

It was about then when RaeJon arrived.

RAEJON:

Daddy! Daddy! Daddy!

VOICE IN CROWD:

His daddy was awful good to that boy and his brother.

ANOTHER VOICE IN CROWD:

Put 'em both through the college.

RAEJON:

Daddy! Daddy! Oh God, poor Daddy! (*Turns to those around.*) Two hours ago, Momma called. She woke and he just wasn't there beside her. My wife and me and Momma and my two girls, we been shoutin' and walkin' all about the land. Don't know how he got this far.

. . . They toted RaeJon's daddy into the ambulance, which pulled away with its lights flashing and siren whickle-whacking. But that commotion stopped nearly right away. Preacher thought he saw the woman in the ambulance reach over and flip all that mess off, shaking her head at the young male driver. 'I gotta go get Momma,' RaeJon said, his shoulders relaxing after the whickle-whacking stopped. He wiped his eyes and nodded. And then he drove off in one of his miniature transportation buses. 'That dog got its rabies shot?' the tall town cop asked. 'It ain't nowhere near old enough,' the Black sheriff deputy interrupted, giving Preacher a look of 'What can you do?' 'You find my green bandana in your truck, let me know,' Gene's Towing Service said. 'I will,' Preacher promised.

BOY IN CROWD:

Go on and tell us about that girlie you found by the tracks. Was she pretty?

ANOTHER BOY IN CROWD:

Was she naked when you found her? Someone shoot or strangle her?

GIRL IN CROWD:

Some man do something bad to her?

LIZZIE, GIRL POET IN CROWD:

Young crow puff out, 'I spy more dead meat than you.'
Old possum snort and give two bones a chomp.
'Young crow, young crow, you do speak true,
But mine tastes best 'cause I drag it through swamp.'

... Back then, Preacher drove a robin's egg blue Ford pickup that he'd inherited from his father. 'Ford. Fixed Or Repaired Daily,' his father'd always complained. But that wasn't true. The Ford was dependable and its six cylinders were easy on the gas. Still, Preacher traded the blue pickup in for a black one after he found the girl by the tracks. It seemed right.

For some reason, as he crossed the tracks that long time ago morning, he looked to his right and spotted a girl slumped and lying beside a crumpled metal switching box. He pulled over and ran on back. 'You okay? You need—' But he stopped because her both eyes were open, staring just over his shoulder like she'd spied an old friend. And her mouth hung down in wonder. One dirty white palm lay up, one turned over in a fist clutching at something, gravel on the railroad track's bed, maybe. He didn't have a cell phone back then, not everyone did. He slowed and walked closer toward her. Her dress was so dirty he couldn't tell its color. Yellow? Light blue? Gray? Her skinny legs crisscrossed. Torn tennis shoes, same non-color as the dress. How old was she? Sixteen? Seventeen? Nineteen? He couldn't tell. Anyways, not a whole lot younger than him back then. He bent and shooed away a green-yellow fly, and then another, a gray-black one with bulbous red eyes and prickly hairy spines sticking out. He bent and opened her hand, which wasn't yet stiff. It held a firefly that flew off, blinking once in the lambent morning air.

Preacher looked around, and then back to the highway. He needed to stop someone and have them call the police while he stayed here and kept away the flies and the buzzards and raccoons that might eat at her. She deserved that much, didn't she? He swatted another buzzing fly and accidentally patted her matted brown hair. Her head twisted so that now she looked at him. 'Preacher,' he heard her think-say. 'Don't leave me out here all alone.' 'How'd you know my name?' 'I know everything now,' she replied. He backed off and ran the thirty feet to the highway. He stood out in the middle, looking both ways. A dusty white truck came, driving toward the town. Preacher stood in the lane, waving his arms wild-like. The truck looked like it wasn't going to stop, but it did, not more than a foot from Preacher, who ran over to the driver's side. Only to skid backwards when he saw the barrel of a gun pointed at him. 'What you actin' a fool for, boy?' 'There's a girl over there by that metal relay. She's dead. Someone needs to call the police.' The Black man's eyes narrowed at Preacher's words. 'She White,' the woman next to the Black man driving said, her face staying turned into her window. 'You take care of White business, we take care of Black. Move!' The man waved the barrel, and Preacher jumped back as the truck laid rubber and bounced over the railroad tracks. Watching the truck's rear end, Preacher realized that he'd peed his pants.

A red car came and its driver swerved to avoid Preacher, rushing on by. Finally a man in a green pickup stopped. Preacher told him about the dead girl. The man looked over, nodded, and reached down. Preacher jumped back, thinking someone else was going to pull a gun on him, but the man had a CB radio installed and he used it to call the sheriff.

LIZZIE, GIRL POET IN CROWD:

When you're dead and your eyes go gone,
That's when you see the most.
Your brain flaps over rivers each day long,
To learn the world, from coast to coast.

PREACHER:

No, the girl wasn't shot or strangled or stabbed. She wasn't naked. The coroner said she died of malnutrition and loneliness. He said when they took her in, all four of her pockets were filled with fireflies, most of them dead, though some flew off alive. He said fireflies were stuffed in the band of her skirt, too. She wasn't wearing any jewelry and didn't carry anything but those fireflies. Hundreds of them, the coroner said, maybe a thousand. They put out pictures of her all over the cop wire Internet, but they never got an identification reply. Folks around here started calling her

The Fairy Girl, because of all the fireflies. For a week of nights I lay awake in my daddy's house and imagined her running along the railroad tracks, hopping and jumping to catch them. I'd see her holding a firefly out to me and then singing soft-like, *You weren't the one to die. You weren't the one to die. Why? Why?* That's when I traded my blue truck in for a black. That's when I sold my daddy's house.

WOMAN IN CROWD:

A person oughtn't sell what is rightly given him.

BOY IN CROWD:

If she was a fairy, did you steal her wand?

GIRL IN CROWD:

If she was a fairy did she smooch on other women?

ANOTHER BOY IN CROWD:

Did she stuff the fireflies down in her panties? What color were they?

WOMAN IN CROWD:

I don't like it that that ambulance woman said this was the highway to hell. It ain't that way. We got the world's longest yard sale every October on it. Nice folk stop by from states off. Every October.

PREACHER:

Finally, they put a little cross over her grave, which was just marked 'Unknown' and the year of her death and 'Found along Highway 28 West beside railroad tracks.' Later, someone hung up a wood plaque that said, 'The Fairy Girl.'

. . . After that, Preacher began to drink. He tried going to a big university up in the city, but drink collared him there too and made him come back. Then there were others that Preacher found. Sometimes he thought it was just like the tall city cop said, even before the tall city cop said it, that Preacher was walking, talking Bad Luck for other folk.

Preacher found the bled-out man in an old barn, staring up at an empty hayloft.

He found the girl drowned in her car after a flash flood, her face smushed against the driver's window like a kiss.

He'd found his own father. Preacher had made coffee and walked out to the front porch. He sat down and began talking about the heat already beating down. His father's rocker didn't move. Preacher said, 'Remember how Momma loved those pink azaleas.' His father's rocker didn't move. 'Daddy?' His father's rocker didn't move.

And then the man in Lake Blue, whose boat had turned over, whose fishing tackle and string of still alive crappie had wrapped around him, flapping and slapping his face.

And then the little boy on the bike with training wheels who'd waved at Preacher until the car behind ran over his bike and him.

PREACHER:

But listen, folks, Pup changed all that. I thought about naming her 'Lucky,' but I didn't.

WOMAN IN CROWD:

That's what my little boy named his pit bull that got stolen. 'Lucky.' I'm sayin' you're the one that—

MAN IN CROWD:

Jane, Jane. He just a while back told us he found that puppy. He didn't steal your son's puppy.

WOMAN IN CROWD:

Just look at his eyes. He did it. (*She angrily faces Preacher, leaning and holding up a fist.*) Tell the truth!

PREACHER:

Truth? There's no one alive knows that.

. . . So Preacher and Pup went out riding of a Saturday. Fall was coming. Leaves were catching in the wind to make little swirlies. Pup would run at them and bark. Or if she was in the truck, she would stand at the window and bark. Preacher stopped at a pullover, and he and Pup got out to stretch. Up ahead, around two curves, Preacher knew, lay the railroad track and the metal relay that someone had wrecked into, twisting it sideways. The railroad had never fixed it over the years, because they didn't use the track that much anymore. Maybe the Fairy Girl had thought it was a skewed little cozy cabin to sleep beside.

Pup was yipping. There were two pecan trees by the road where they'd stopped. People'd be coming and gathering pecans in plastic grocery bags in a couple of weeks. There was a squirrel in one of the trees, chittering at Pup below. The squirrel hopped from limb to limb, chittering on, while Pup jumped at the bark of the pecan tree, tongue lolling out, bark scattering off. Then the squirrel fell out of the tree. Preacher'd never seen a squirrel fall before, didn't know they could. But supposedly angels had fallen, so why not squirrels, he thought. The squirrel ran across the highway, Pup ran after it, and Preacher ran after Pup. Gene's Towing Service was slinging along the road. He braked hard and went off into a small ditch. The squirrel and Pup ran on. Preacher caught his breath, and Gene's Towing Service wiped his brow with a dark green bandana just like the one Pup had chewed up. 'Glad I didn't run that squirrel and your puppy and you over,' Gene's Towing Service said. 'I hate to see things die on this road. It's a waste.'

BOY IN CROWD:

I wish that ditch had been forty-foot deep and he'd turned over to crunch his skull. He's mean and fat.

WOMAN IN CROWD:

He's not fat. He's handsome and muscled and tall. He helped my momma and my daddy once. Didn't even ask 'em for money.

. . . Gene's Towing Service opened his truck door and told Preacher that he'd found a replacement bandana that was nearly as lucky as the old one he'd lost. 'Was hoping it would turn up in your truck, maybe,' Gene's Towing Service said. 'I went back to the spot you'd stalled out, couldn't find it, though. That's okay, this one's as good. It'll maybe even bring more luck. That's why I didn't hit anyone just now, that's why I just ran off the highway a bit and no damage.'

So it turned out that both Preacher and Gene's Towing Service had found some bit of luck. That's how it seemed. Gene's Towing Service backed out of the small ditch and Preacher called Pup to him. The squirrel had already skittered away.

SELF-APPOINTED SPOKESMAN:

Thought you told us that all would fall. That's what you said, 'All will fall.' And then you got mad because we laughed. Well maybe now we'll laugh again, 'cause you're trying to sell us this silly good luck stuff. Ain't none, never was, especially along this highway. Never will be.

PREACHER:

You remember I told you about the moon and the sun, their second bet?

SELF-APPOINTED SPOKESMAN:

Yeah, so what?

PREACHER:

Just remember, that's all.

Sea Change, or, The Truth

. . . Some folk like chocolate pudding, some like vanilla. Some dogs like water, some stick to dry land. Pup loved water. 'Pup, she loves her some water and swimming,' Preacher said one supper hour at the boxing plant. He bit into a bologna and mustard sandwich and chewed. 'I got a pond that's almost as big as a lake on my property,' an older man Preacher'd made friends with said. 'You can bring your dog out anytime. People fish it some, but there ain't no bass. Just bluegill and cat.' 'I been wondering,' an anxious young man who'd just started work there, who swayed back and forth whenever he spoke, he said this. 'I been wondering, could we build boxes for people? I mean to bury them in. It'd be lots cheaper, wouldn't it? Should I tell the supervisor and get a raise?' The older man with the big pond looked at the young man, who barely came up to the other two men's vestigial nipples. 'Son, you don't want no cut-rate funeral. No one does. Funeral's the only dignity a lot of people get.'

PREACHER:

So Pup and me and our new good luck rode out to that big pond the next weekend. The weather was nice for once, not too hot, a fine blue north Alabama sky, some birds now and then. It reminded me of a girl I once dated. Yes ma'ams, I did date once. She happened in my life before people started calling me Preacher. She was sweet as a plump fistful of blueberries growing under a big wide oak tree. But her parents moved because of a new job her dad got, and she left out to go with them. I think maybe then was when people started calling me 'Preacher.' I didn't preach or anything. I guess I just looked sad. (*PREACHER here shakes his head and studies his boots.*)

SELF-APPOINTED SPOKESMAN IN CROWD:

We ain't got time for your moping, Preacher. Get on with your tale.

PREACHER:

Out at the pond, Pup saw a fish jump in the water. She skidded into the water after it, splashing up everywhere. I'd bought two Cokes and two cheese sandwiches, so I settled down and watched Pup. The lettuce had wilted, so I threw it in the water. A fish swam up and plucked it. That water was like the day, perfect. It wasn't leaving out anywhere. I thought how everyone's life should be just like that day, clear and sunshiny. I heard something on the other side of the pond, which was large, like the man at the boxing plant said, almost a lake. A hundred or more yards away, that other side lay off. A boy and a girl were swimming and splashing in the water over there. Pup stayed too intent on the fishes and the water to care, but I watched them with a clear and sunshiny smile. My friend at work had three boys, so I guessed this was the oldest, just ready to go to college or get a job.

Splashing, splashing, the boy and the girl were. And Pup, she was splashing, too. I thought maybe I'd join and get in the real shallow part and cool off with some splashes, even though I was afraid of water. I glanced to the beautiful sky. Of sudden, the girl screamed. The boy screamed. I couldn't swim, so I ran around the lake-pond, yanking at my cell phone. Pup shook herself and ran after me.

I watched the boy holding something up out of the water—a snake. It stuck at his face, and the boy let it go. I couldn't see the girl. I ran. Pup ran. I called 911 and then the man who owned the pond. I ran. I couldn't swim. People got there, but too late.

What kind of God-plan is it that lets two young kids meet up with a nest of mating water moccasins while a puppy and a man who can't swim watch? Not clear and sunshiny, not clear and sunshiny.

WOMAN IN CROWD:

You shouldn't question God. He knows things we don't know.

MAN IN CROWD:

Satan first appeared as a snake. It's Satan does all the bad things. Him and wicked men.

ANOTHER WOMAN IN CROWD:

How wicked can two teenagers be? Preacher's right. There's something wrong, somehow. Maybe God makes mistakes.

LIZZIE, GIRL POET IN CROWD:

God's a great potter, throwing his pots.
Some he likes, some he does not.
Some he keeps, some he lets drop.
"Tough luck," he grumbles, "for any with spots."

WOMAN IN CROWD:

It's not that way, you hateful girl! Jesus loves us all! It's not that way! I don't see why you don't go off somewhere and spout your poetry and die in hellfire! Jesus loves us all!

ANOTHER WOMAN IN CROWD:

Agnes, Agnes, be calm. Think.

WOMAN IN CROWD:

I don't need to think. Thinking's what's so bad with the world and that hateful girl.

. . . For four days, Preacher wouldn't go back to work at the boxing plant, for fear he'd see the man who owned the pond who'd lost his son partly because Preacher couldn't swim. On the fifth day, a Friday, Preacher heard steps on his porch and then a knock. 'It's me, Preacher, Todd.' 'And his wife, Elsa, too.' 'We want to talk with you, Preacher.' 'We want to hear what our boy was doing, before all that happened.' 'It would be a comfort, Preacher, to know that him and his sweet girl were happy.' 'Yes, and that they were having fun, like kids are supposed to be having.' The woman named Elsa whimpered when she said this. Through his front door screen, Preacher could see her shoulders shaking.

So he asked them in, and Pup ran around them yipping. Todd's wife Elsa bent to pet Pup, and she laughed a short laugh. Preacher told them about their son and the girl. He told them that he'd watched them playing and laughing for over an hour. He told them that they walked over and threw a bright green tennis ball for Pup to fetch. He told them that they would sneak an innocent kiss when they thought he and Pup weren't looking. He told, he told. He told, he told, he told.

ELSA:

He was going to graduate in two months from high school. They'd been going together all through high school, never broke up like other kids.

TODD:

Like his two brothers.

ELSA:

Yes, like his two brothers did. We thought and hoped for sure that our oldest and his girl'd get married right after graduation, that he'd set an example to his brothers.

PREACHER:

I . . . he . . .

ELSA

I knew it! Did you see him propose to her? I told you, Todd, that's what he was taking her out there for! I had a feeling.

PREACHER:

He got down on his knees and held her hand and looked up at her wet face shining in the clear sunlight. Pup ran to jump and lick and paw on them both. I saw her smile—a big smile, a huge smile. And I watched her nod and wipe a tear from her eyes. She was a pretty girl. Your boy was a handsome boy.

ELSA:

Oh, I knew it. I just knew it.

PREACHER: (*Looking out at the crowd: some wipe their own eyes, some look puzzled, some gaze off to a cloud passing overhead with an intent hawk whirling under it, looking for something to snatch.*) After the lake-pond, I knew my luck hadn't really changed at all. But there in my kitchen, I caught up Pup and gave Todd and Elsa some pork and beans I'd baked. I told them how I'd seen their oldest boy kneel to propose to that girl, how she'd taken his hands and danced a spinning dance around him as she looked down with pure love in her eyes. Todd, he spotted a can of Vienna Sausages on the counter and asked if he could put those in his beans. 'Sure,' I said. Todd gave one little sausage to Pup, who was starting to learn to sit. They stayed half an hour more and then they left. Todd's wife, Elsa, took both of my hands and squeezed. 'It was like God sent you to that pond to see all that,' she said, blinking back a tear. I nodded.

LIZZIE, GIRL POET IN CROWD:

As the great wheel turns, it'll stop and lean.
Some fall, some jump; some laugh, some scream.
Stops in autumn, leaves play red; in spring, emerald green.
In winter, on ground they rot. In summer, they fake a sheen.

WOMAN IN CROWD:

I just wish you'd shut up. You make my head hurt, trying to understand your so-called poetry.

MOTHER IN CROWD:

Let her be. She's trying to help us all in her own way.

ANOTHER WOMAN IN CROWD:

That man up there standing on that table is a liar. You just heard. And he stole my boy's puppy, too!

MAN IN CROWD:

I wouldn't doubt it. He rides around with your son's dog in that black pick-up like he's king of the county, smoking those big cigars.

ANOTHER WOMAN IN CROWD:

Cigarettes ain't good enough for him.

PREACHER:

I've never told you about my mother. She was a nurse in a war. That's when she met my father, though he wasn't wounded like you'd think. They were swimming at a beach by a river or ocean or lake. It was . . . it was a clear and sunshiny day. They weren't supposed to be swimming there. But they were young and wild with war and hormones.

BOY IN CROWD:

Hey! You know how to make a whore moan?

GIRL IN CROWD:

Shut up, Willy. Gross. You're immature. We want to hear about his mother and the war.

PREACHER:

They were young and wild. There were a couple dozen of them, nurses and soldiers. Swimming and splashing, lying on the sand, admiring one another, like men and women do. Of sudden, one of them just coming out of the water jerked and fell. They heard the shot. An enemy sniper on a cliff, they guessed. Dad said that he pulled Momma behind a rock. Momma said Daddy got so busy looking for his gun—they all at least paid that much attention to the war, to bring their guns, that is—that he almost got shot, too. The sniper wasn't all that good. This shot of his thwacked up the sand a foot or more from Daddy. Momma said she was the one pulled Daddy behind the rock. (*Preacher pauses here and looks out at the men and women and children and babes in arms in the crowd before him.*) They both were smart, tough old birds, so I doubt either one of them needed much pulling. Someone got a bead on the sniper and killed him. Daddy and two other guys climbed up to make sure he was dead. Daddy got a knife the sniper was carrying. I still have it. I don't suppose many of you . . . (*Preacher pauses and looks out over the crowd again. He shifts on the picnic table and it creaks. He searches under the table and calls something and then looks up.*) I don't suppose maybe *any* of you ever met my momma. She died eight months after we moved here. Daddy always said it was from the Highway 28 blues.

WOMAN IN CROWD:

It be a bluesome place, sure enough.

HER FRIEND IN CROWD:

Amen, sister.

ANOTHER WOMAN IN CROWD:

I told you all we got the World's Longest Yard Sale. People stop by from nearly every state except Hawaii, maybe even there sometime.

PREACHER:

I been here most of my life.

MAN IN CROWD:

You weren't born here.

WOMAN IN CROWD:

That's right. You weren't born here like us. Just 'cause you dated that Jenkins' girl who moved away don't give you no special knowledge. You need to be born here to appreciate.

PREACHER:

After Todd and Elsa left, I looked at Pup, who started whimpering and scratching at the front door. I heard Todd's truck start up and leave, crunching gravel to the gate. 'All right, Pup. I guess you're right. We need to get on out and see what's happening in the world.' I said this, understand, but my lungs and heart fell heavy, dropping down beneath my soles to the sticky yellow kitchen linoleum. My luck had changed back to bad, no doubt about it. I was fearful of what Pup and me would run into out there.

WOMAN IN CROWD:

Why didn't you just pull your feet off that linoleum, go crunch some gravel and ride out from that gate to sleep and live in a graveyard? Snuggle up in a coffin? (*The crowd hoots and laughs.*)

LIZZIE, GIRL POET IN CROWD:

The grave's a sad and private place,
I bet that no one hastes to race
And hop right in. We'd rather stay and wait,
'Cept those whose cup gets filled with hate.

WOMAN IN CROWD:

I swear to the Good Lord above, girl. Jesus is going to strike you one of these days.

ANOTHER WOMAN IN CROWD:

Jesus loves us all, doesn't he? Why're you wishing hate on this little girl?

WOMAN IN CROWD:

She ain't little. Old enough to have a baby. Slutty enough too, from her looks.

MOTHER IN CROWD:

My Lizzie's no slut! She studies hard in school and minds her own business. She's just trying to help us understand. You want a slut, look around in your own back yard.

SELF-APPOINTED SPOKESMAN:

Let's calm down and listen to what Preacher's got to say. No need to quarrel.

PREACHER:

So Pup kept at it, scratching on the door until I grabbed an iced-tea for me and water for Pup, and we loaded into the pick-up.

… This day was supposed to rain, according to the weather that Preacher'd heard the night before. But the sky was just gray, lots and lots of plain old gray, just as far as Preacher and Pup could see. Gray, gray, gray. He and Pup loaded into the truck, crunched over gravel and drove on out. It was a Friday. Todd had brought him his check from work, so he went to the bank to cash some of it.

MAN IN CROWD:

Banks is what's driving this country to hell. Every time you turn around they charge you for something else, all just to shuffle your money! None of 'em do any real work. Hell, they even got machines to count the money. Don't want to get them milky fingers dirty.

PREACHER:

The teller at the drive-in window was so pretty, with her freckles and bunched red and wispy hair. It was like she'd hopped off the boat from Ireland to come here and be happy and make a living. With my new returned bad luck, I thought, 'Oh no, don't make it her.' But she just smiled a crooked smile at me and Pup. She even gave Pup a dog biscuit, which he ate right up and which reminded me that me and Pup hadn't eaten much of those baked beans, since Todd and Elsa had turned so happy-hungry when I talked about how their son and that girl had danced in a great wide circle under the clear and shining sun. Well, I felt so good after leaving the bank window and that red-headed Irish teller and listening to Pup crunch that dog biscuit that I thought maybe a leprechaun had jumped into the truck right from her window. That maybe she'd seen how sad me and Pup looked with our new bad luck and tossed the leprechaun in from her pot of gold.

It was fall then, and folks were out planting cover crops or turning over whatever hadn't grown all that hardy because of no rain. I passed three farmers on tractors, the enclosed air-conditioned kind, so they couldn't hear even if Pup barked and I honked. But I waved anyway. It never hurts to spread a smile and a wave.

WOMAN IN CROWD:

Even if you're the deputy of Death? Even if that black pickup of yours is a rolling hearse gathering bodies?

ANOTHER WOMAN IN CROWD:

Even if you drive around stealing puppies?

MAN IN CROWD:

Jane, isn't your son up north in college now? Shouldn't you just move on and let that lost puppy dog go?

WOMAN IN CROWD:

It wasn't lost. He up there stole it.

PREACHER:

Pup and me were at the edge of the city. The high school's football field showed just ahead, its stadium with its picture of the mascot in the afternoon sun—

WOMAN IN CROWD:

Oh no, don't talk about that day, please. I can't stand to hear it anymore, evermore. Never. Never. Please don't. *(Another woman in the crowd places her arms around the first woman's shoulders as they tremble.)*

PREACHER:

'See, Pup. That's you up there on that big drawing on the stadium.' I said this and reached over to pat Pup's haunch. '*Pit Bulls. We won't let go,*' I read off to Pup. My truck's windows were both down since it was leafy and fall. Pup raised her ears, and soon after I heard the sound of cheers. They were having a pep rally for the game—

WOMAN IN CROWD:

Please stop. Please make him stop.

SELF-APPOINTED SPOKESMAN IN CROWD:

We got to hear it, Louise. It's gotta be told.

WOMAN IN CROWD:

Why? Why? Why can't we just hear breathing and laughing and chewing and sneezing?

ANOTHER WOMAN IN CROWD:

Why can't we just hear praying?

MAN IN CROWD:

What kind of praying?

WOMAN IN CROWD:

Does it matter what kind?

MAN IN CROWD:

You bet it does. You want some Moslem or Jew praying to your God?

ANOTHER MAN IN CROWD:

Want some Latter-Day-Mormon praying?

. . . Preacher wondered if they'd let him in to watch the rally and all the kids jumping and whooping. Probably not, he decided, since schools were so scared of strangers these days. Of sudden, he saw flashes from atop the stands. Pup whimpered and Preacher heard *Pop! Pop! . . . Pop! Pop! Pop!* And even more *Pops!* They came like they would never stop. And then the screams. The band kept playing its silly oompah tubas and rat-tatting drums—but for only maybe three or four seconds. Or maybe even just one or two. And then only *Pop! Pop! . . . Pop! Pop! Pop!*

And the screams. And the flashes. And the screams. And the flashes.

LIZZIE, GIRL POET IN CROWD:

Death has tiny toes and tiny feet,
Has claws for hands, and bones for arms.
Whenever it walks, it sneaks soft and neat.
Whenever it grabs—too late for alarm.

PREACHER:

There were nineteen wounded and four killed. All those *Pop! Pops!* I swerved on in past the guard station. The guard wasn't there. I thought maybe he'd run toward those shots. Then I thought maybe he'd run the other direction to hide from those shots. The boy, had he just driven on by the guard and climbed up the high bleacher steps? Had he climbed and retrieved a rifle and ammunition he'd hidden there the night before? Had someone spit ice at him as he climbed? Had two girls laughed at him? Had the boy just looked their way and smiled a crooked smile? *Pop! Pop! . . . Pop! Pop! Pop!*

Pup and me could see the boy up there on top of the stadium's bleachers, aiming that rifle. He dropped out a clip and inserted another. Pup barked and I honked. We barked and honked and the boy turned to look. He shot at us, but he didn't even hit the truck. It was like he was that sniper on top of that cliff shooting half-assed at my daddy and momma, except even worse. He didn't even hit my truck. I blew the horn again. Pup barked. He shot again. He managed to hit the windshield of a car parked nearby. I heard a *Pop!* Then wailing sirens from everywhere. I jumped out of the truck. I yelled up at the boy, '*Stop it, stop it!*' Pup ran after me, barking. '*Stop it, stop it, stop it!*' I yelled. The boy shot three times. Another windshield behind me, two dirt splashes in front of me. '*Why don't you just jump! Jump! You're a coward! Jump!*' And then the boy tumbled, his rifle *Pop! Popping!* twice before he hit the ground giving a bounce and a roll. So. Nineteen wounded and five dead. Later, a coach and a football player said they ran up and pushed him. I don't know. Later, people said the boy was angry because a cheerleader didn't love him, because the students and even the teachers made fun of him because of his drippy nose. Threw ice at him. I don't know.

WOMAN IN CROWD:

You yelled up at that poor confused boy to jump?!

PREACHER:

The words just came. They . . . they jumped from my mouth. I didn't mean them. I did mean them. They jumped from my mouth just like he jumped from that top row in the stadium. I wanted him to stop shooting his classmates and teachers. I was studying part-time in tech school on getting an EMT license. I thought to help someone someday, instead of just . . . maybe that coach did push him. I don't know.

. . . They wouldn't let Preacher in to help, even though he told them he was taking classes in EMT. But he didn't have to go in to see the four bodies, to hear the four hundred and four screams. And he'd already seen the boy's crushed body outside. So he drove off, but something at the guardhouse made him stop, maybe a buzzing of flies, maybe an oozing pool of blood, maybe two empty brass cartridges on the blacktop, shiny and hot in the sun. He got out and looked inside. The guard lay cattywampus behind a metal stool.

His eyes looked somewhere else, but it was his face, his smile that caught Preacher. It was the same crooked smile the Irish teller had. It was like the guard had watched the boy pull out a pistol. It was like the guard had opened his arms to the boy's two bullets, saying, 'It's about time. Where have you been these three years since my wife died?' So. Nineteen wounded, six dead. Behind, at the stadium, the screams had turned to wails. Pup began to howl.

WOMAN IN CROWD:

Why don't you just move on? Take your damned Pup with you and just move on. Look how you've upset Louise. Her two twin girls were both shot and killed by that crazy boy. Lots of kids round here wake up screaming of a night, even though they're adults, some with children of their own now. Why don't you just move on? Leave us be.

SELF-APPOINTED SPOKESMAN IN CROWD:

We've got to hear it all. We need to hear him out. It's . . . it's . . . just . . . it's something we all have got—

WOMAN IN CROWD:

And why is that, I ask again? Why do we gotta hear it? Look at Louise. (*She moves to put her arms around the woman named Louise. Others move in with her. They all glare at Preacher.*)

SELF-APPOINTED SPOKESMAN:

There is no why. We just do.

... Preacher and Pup walked back to tell a policeman about the guard. There were ambulances from all around, four or five counties. Who'd pay for their services, Preacher wondered. Death was expensive. Could the school or the city or the state just put it on a MasterCard? Maybe the ambulances would be like Gene's Towing Service and not take American Express.

Preacher half-expected Gene's Towing Service to show at the high school, maybe to haul the kid's car away. Maybe to haul the guard's truck away. There were lots of cars that needed hauling away. But after taking a cop and two EMTs to the guardhouse and watching the EMTs put their two fingers on the guard's neck to say what everyone knew, Preacher and Pup just drove out alone, turning to the right on Highway 28 West. Preacher thought maybe he'd drive until the sun set. That maybe he'd drive all weekend until it was time to go to work at the boxing plant.

Driving eased thinking, because you had to watch the road. Driving was the modern day Buddhism. It was nirvana. It was No-Mind. Preacher turned the steering wheel along a curve to the right. He leaned to the center and Pup leaned to the door. Preacher turned the steering wheel along a curve to the left. He leaned to the door and Pup leaned to the center. Nirvana.

Preacher put in a CD of Mississippi John Hurt. Hurt was singing 'Payday.' *Well, a rabbit in a log. Ain't got no rabbit dog. Lord, I hate to see that rabbit get away.* Does everything always get away, Preacher wondered. Why can't I play guitar and sing like John Hurt, Preacher wondered. 'Because you're too busy riding around finding dead people,' he answered himself aloud.

MAN IN CROWD:

What happened to your damned Buddha nirvana hocus-pocus?

PREACHER:

It got away.

. . . Preacher turned the steering wheel along a curve to the right. He leaned toward the center and Pup leaned toward the door. Then Preacher turned the steering wheel along a curve to the left. He leaned toward the door and Pup leaned toward the center. But now it wasn't Buddhism or nirvana descending. It was this: *What's lying around that coming curve? Is this going to be the curve that turns up another dead body? Are Pup and me going to have to get out and sniff another dead body? Give a sniff and put two fingers to its carotid and nod?*

WOMAN IN CROWD:

Leave! Leave! Get out of this town! (*Two friends grab her. She almost topples them before letting out a banshee wail that leaves the air still and anxious. Then it lowers and makes the wavy air lean forward and look. After maybe a minute, a distant hollow thud sounds, maybe some child hitting a fifty-gallon drum with a metal pipe, maybe someone firing a shotgun. The thud comes from too far away to be sure.)*

PREACHER:

Pup and me drove. I forgot my halfway rule until Pup began panting for water. I reached back and pulled out a bottle and poured some in a little bowl I keep. I drank the rest. We drove. For two hours or more, it seemed that police cars and ambulances never stopped passed us heading for the high school stadium, their sirens and lights never stopping. Then evening came. I saw a yellow light in a house, blinking like a signal. I slowed. Maybe someone needed my help. Maybe I could stop and give them some water, too. I'd found another bottle.

WOMAN IN CROWD: *(Screaming.)*

Your help?! You're the Devil! You're Satan! Death is all you know!

PREACHER:

I'd taken two EMT courses, was taking a third. I didn't want to stand for the exam and become one because I already had a good boxing plant job. I just wanted to know how to help folks. I wanted to kneel beside them and help them. I pulled off the road. The yellow light was still blinking. It was one of those bug lights. 'Come on, Pup,' I said. 'Someone might need our help.'

WOMAN IN CROWD: (*Screams again, incoherently. Two other women rush to hold her.*)

. . . Pup and Preacher walked on the dirt driveway leading to the blinking yellow light and the shack that just squatted and stared. It came dark all around, no real light, no sound, no smell. Maybe dew in the air formed on Preacher's skin. Maybe a gnat, maybe a mosquito bit him or buzzed in his ear. Preacher stumbled in a hole, so he pulled out a small flashlight.

BOY IN CROWD:

Why didn't you just use your fancy new cell phone? They got lights on them, you know.

. . . Preacher and Pup walked on, quickening the pace now that they could see. Preacher had a feeling that someone needed help. That blinking light was an S. O. S. And there he would be because all the ambulances and police and doctors and nurses and even firemen were still back at the school stadium. There was a wooden porch in front of the shack. It clonked hollow when Preacher stepped on it. The front door was open, and it seemed that the simple force of Preacher and Pup stepping toward it eased it open some more. 'Anyone home?' Preacher called. Pup gave a small yip. 'Anyone home? You need help? I saw your blinking yellow light.'

He called a couple more times and shined his flashlight inside the shack. There was a tattered brown couch on the left wall. There were two wood chairs and a card table. Something skittered along the dusty floor. Preacher sneezed and then leaned. The inside of the shack smelled like cheese. *Oh Lord*, he thought, *someone is dying of gangrene*. He thought this because of the second EMT class. 'Anyone home? You need some help?' The yellow porch light behind him kept blinking. Maybe half a mile away down the highway, a dog howled. Pup whimpered. Preacher's flashlight showed another room. He walked into it through the open arched doorway. There was a wooden table, and on it sat a folded piece of paper that made a tent. *Come another day*, the handwritten note on the paper read. There were chalky white cabinets to the right and to the left. Most of their doors were open, and most of the cabinets held nothing. There was a large spider's web in one, chewed cardboard in another, like a mouse had just run off. A wood-burning stove squatted to the rear of the room. There was another door leading out. Preacher could see through that door's hazy window. He could see that what looked like an old, old outhouse was all that stood in the back yard. No, there was a clothesline too, one of those merry-go-round kind that twirl from a single metal pole. Ring around the rosy. He walked and put his nose against the door's glass. Behind him, the yellow light kept blinking. And in front of him too because its blinks reflected in the dirty window and on the peeling white paint of the door. He tried the back door's knob, which was locked, as if someone wanted to keep someone else inside the house, as a prisoner. Maybe a crazy person that needed locking up. Maybe the crazy person had busted through the front door after leaving the mysterious short note. Preacher walked back and made sure that was all it said, *Come another day*. Yep, it was. But it wasn't written like a crazy person's writing, because it was precise and followed a line, as if someone had used ruled paper to guide their fingers. But then really, maybe that really did mean that they really were crazy. It could, couldn't it? Being so particular about things like handwritten notes, that is. And then he noticed what might have been an initial below the single precise sentence, which had a period after it. Terribly formal for a kitchen table note, Preacher thought. *J* was the initial. John? Jim? Joe? Jeff? Jesus? Judas? Or maybe Jessica. Or maybe Jolene. Didn't have to be a male. Didn't have to be a female. Well, he guessed it had to be one or the other. Or maybe not. Maybe it was a Q for 'Questioning.' Johnnie? Johnny? Jerry? Jeri? Joe? Jo?

    Preacher and Pup left the shack and got into their truck. The sky above was black except for stars. The sun and the moon, they'd had enough for the day. The high school stadium had filled them plenty. Preacher searched for the Milky Way. There. Wobbling through the nighttime sky. He saluted it. Milk, mother's nourishing milk, but so very far away, through all that black space. So very far away. He and Pup drove back to eat. A long weekend faced them and the town.

PREACHER:

I went to school once . . .

MAN IN CROWD:

We heard all about you down there in Tuscaloosa, drinkin' and slobberin' and pawin'. (*Laughter.*)

WOMAN IN CROWD:

That's right, Preacher. We heard plenty of stories. Don't try to one-up and confuse us with book matter.

PREACHER:

I went to school, and that's where I learned that Math rules the world, the sun, the moon, the stars, the Milky Way.

ANOTHER WOMAN IN CROWD:

That's blasphemy.

PREACHER:

The sun, the moon, earth, and all the planets and stars. Math rules everything because Math says, 'Stop and take a look around. There are so many other ways you can be. Don't you want that? To be one of those other things? To be something else? Chaos. Wouldn't you like that? Go for it. So many other random ways. Go ahead, fall apart, scatter. That's the only real, that's the real way you're meant to be. Life's not a ruled piece of paper. You don't need that. You don't want that. Go for it. Skit. Scat. Fall apart. There now, there now. Don't cry. That's my eternal, my only commandment.' And then Math folds its ten arms atop one another, gathering them in with an abacus's clack. And then Math waits, no grin on its face, no frown, no nothing.

Next day was a Saturday. I woke up and scrambled six eggs for me and Pup. Pup licked the skillet clean and I washed it and hung it up on a nail on the wall. 'Years, Pup,' I announced. Pup tilted her head. 'Years are what we have.' We didn't drive anywhere that day. We just mowed the lawn in straight lines and pretended we were normal with a nicely manicured lawn, filled with nicely even and lemony green grass.

. . . And the days came, and the months came, and the years came. The moon and the sun danced their tango or their waltz. They made their bets, keeping them secret from the stars, from everyone. Preacher went to work and made boxes. The boy who'd suggested making boxes for coffins died in a car wreck. He'd been drinking with friends. Even though the kid was short, Preacher thought it would be nice to make him a box coffin, but he didn't tell anyone this. He especially didn't tell his friend Todd who owned the pond, who lost his boy and his boy's girl. Preacher just walked out one early, early morning after his shift to the waste pile in back of the plant and grabbed four mis-cut boxes. He carried them to his truck and took them home and duct-taped them together. He put the result on the floor in his kitchen and stared at it. He stared and stared. Two weeks later, he and Pup drove what he'd made and laid it on top of the boy's short grave. The rain would eat the boxes and soak them into the ground and into the boy's bones. 'I think somehow maybe the boy will appreciate that, Pup,' Preacher told Pup, who was beating her tail on yellow flowers that had fallen to wilt. Their petals scattered with each thump of Pup's tail.

PREACHER:

I admit that I became obsessed with that blinking yellow light and that handwritten note that was so neat and straight. 'Come another day,' the note read. So I drove by that shack every day before and after work, though it was two miles out of my way. Sometimes the yellow light was on, sometimes it wasn't. It never blinked though. (*He pauses, scratches his knee, and then looks at the sky, looks under the picnic table.*) Pup was getting big. She weighed fifty-four pounds and wasn't but six and a half months. The lady vet said it wouldn't be good for her to have puppies in her first heat. The lady vet said, 'We got enough stray dogs around as it is anyway. You should get Pup spayed.'

GIRL IN CROWD:

People are what should get neutered and spayed. There's too many mean ones around.

WOMAN IN CROWD:

And just how would you have felt if your momma and your daddy had done that before you were born?

GIRL IN CROWD:

I wouldn't have felt. I wouldn't have felt nothing. That's the point. There'd be no me to be bothered with any feeling. There'd be no me to be sad.

MAN IN CROWD:

There'd be no you to be happy either.

WOMAN IN CROWD:

You and that poet girl should get together and swap your hate.

ANOTHER WOMAN IN CROWD:

She's just being a girl, Pauline. Don't you remember being young?

PREACHER:

I told the lady vet I'd think on it. The lady vet had starey gray eyes that didn't move but just looked. I told those eyes that I'd think on it. Pup looked from her to me. The lady vet petted Pup's head. 'You don't want to be bothered with any male that's just going to run off and leave you to do all the work, do you, Pup?' the lady vet asked in a high voice.

WOMAN IN CROWD:

Now there's the Lord's truth. *(Laughter from women around her.)*

PREACHER:

Did I ever tell you about the hanged man?

TWO BOYS IN CROWD: *(Holding right hands before their crotches.)*

Wow, even better this way. Yeah, man! Ugh, ugh, ugh! Faster, faster, faster! Go! Go! Go! Whoo-hoo!

MAN IN CROWD:

Quit it, you two. It's not funny.

LIZZIE, GIRL POET IN CROWD:

We all lead secret lives.
We all catch wishes from stars.
We hold them, we sift them,
But time only laughs, time only mars.

PREACHER:

Me and Pup went out driving. It was Saturday night. We passed the Dairy Queen. We passed the old Donald Place.

All their lights were on and a dozen cars were parked in the drive. It looked like they were having a party. We passed the Tigers & Monkeys Bar. People were already in there, trying to forget. We were coming toward the town. We saw the Holy Spirit Catholic Church ahead.

WOMAN IN CROWD:

I still say that foul man was taking advantage of young boys. They all do.

MAN IN CROWD:

Mary, that Catholic Church only has 92 members, most of them old. There can't be more than five boys. Don't you think they'd know if that was going on?

WOMAN IN CROWD:

Maybe they just ignored it. People do that, you know.

PREACHER:

I thought I saw something swinging in the doorway of the church. I thought maybe the priest was out there sweeping or fixing up some special Catholic incense or bells.

WOMAN IN CROWD:

More likely putting up some idolatry on a pedestal for those Catholics to worship.

ANOTHER WOMAN IN CROWD:

That man was strange. Why'd he keep so to himself all the time? I wasn't surprised at all.

THIRD WOMAN IN CROWD:

I'm just glad he didn't get any of our girls pregnant. Their babies would have some 'indelible' mark on their palms or the soles of their feet, I'm certain.

WOMAN IN CROWD:

I'm telling you those priest types don't go for women. They're unnatural. You know what they go for. Unnatural.

PREACHER:

I pulled on in, thought I'd say hello and maybe give him a hand. Father Jackson always had a smile and a pat on the head for Pup.

. . . But Father Jackson wasn't sweeping, he was swaying. Father Jackson had hung himself from the timbering over the front entrance. He'd hung himself at the bleeding feet of Jesus on the Crucifix. A note pinned to Father Jackson's chest read, *Mea Maxima Culpa*. Preacher looked up into Father Jackson's filmed eyes, and Pup barked, jumping at Father Jackson's tennis shoes, which were what he always wore, to the mortification of plenty of the church members. Come each Christmas they bought him a pair of black leather shoes. Come each New Year's he'd be wearing those same tennis shoes. Father Jackson's hands were at his sides, like they were pasted or stapled or glued there. He was dressed up in some clerical doo-dads that were sorrowful and purple. Those colors seemed to match his tennis shoes, which were worn and dirty. Preacher grabbed Father Jackson's cold left hand.

PREACHER:

What's that sign mean, Father?

FATHER JACKSON:

It's Latin. It means, 'My most grievous fault.'

PREACHER:

But what's it mean, Father?

FATHER JACKSON:

It means that for the past nine years I haven't believed, it means that I'm a hypocrite because I've kept telling all these good people that they should believe when I don't.

PREACHER:

But Father—

FATHER JACKSON:

Why should anyone believe? How can anyone believe? You know that. You thought that Pup would change your luck, but she didn't. There's no changed luck on this spinning globe.

PREACHER:

But now and then—

FATHER JACKSON:

That poor woman in the hospital, screaming and looking at her blue baby. Those two poor girls whose father came home drunk and beat them and his wife. Those screaming, dying children at that high school pep rally, that poor misled boy up there shooting them. It's a list, it's a list. Why doesn't God write a different list? How can I believe in Him? And even worse, if I do believe in Him, how can I love him?

PREACHER:

I know, Father. I know.

FATHER JACKSON:

It's all right for you not to believe. You just have Pup. You feed her and pet her and make her as happy as any creature can be in this world. Why would Noah save all those animals, I have to ask. Save them just to start over? Breathing and coughing. Gnashing and being gnashed. Tearing and being torn. Not a flood but a fire next time? And just how is that supposed to comfort? Leave me, just leave me. I was swaying before you came and grabbed my hand. Have Pup jump up and give me a shove. The motion was comforting. A tee-tiny breeze, as my sister used to say. Did I ever tell you I had a sister? Two years older than me. Cecilia, named for the patron saint of musicians, though my sister never played a lick, couldn't even sing. She's somewhere, if she's not dead. She's somewhere with her drugs. Maybe in some hot shack outside some go-nowhere country town. Mosquitoes and flies eating at her in her drug trance stupor, eating at her like she's a special holiday feast. It wouldn't be a moveable one. Why do you think God had to add mosquitoes and flies to the creation mix? How's that create a pluperfect providence? Do you think Noah really meant to save them? Do you think maybe they just hopped a ride on his ark when he wasn't looking?

PREACHER: (*Giving a snort that makes Pup look up.*)

Maybe God has a secret plan. Something we don't know about.

FATHER JACKSON:

Doomsday is the plan, and no one is the planner.

Math Speaks: *Go. Scatter.*

PREACHER:

So many ways to be. You just have to listen when Math speaks: '*So many ways to be. Wouldn't you like to change? Wouldn't you? Chaos, can't you just taste its sweetness in your mouth? Can't you just hear its cling-clanging bells?*'

(*Adopting a falsetto voice.*) Pup, would you like to change? (*Brows furrowing, now in a worried voice.*) Where are you, Pup? (*Preacher looks around the crowd, looks under the table.*) Pup! There you are. You found your ball. (*Pup wags its entire body. Preacher pets it and then looks up.*) Anyway, the police from town came. They looked at the priest, they looked at the note, they looked at me. 'That dog have a rabies tag?' one tall town cop asked. I lifted Pup's collar to show him she did. 'What's that note mean?' the second town cop asked. 'My most grievous fault,' I said. 'Grievous?' the first cop asked. 'Terrible and bad,' I said.

. . . Preacher drove by the shack with the yellow light every night, even when he wasn't working. He'd slow his car so much that he almost got rear-ended twice. Gene's Towing Service would at least get some work, he thought.

And so would the ambulance or the hearse. And the credit card people, they'd make their money, too. It was like everyone was agreeing with Math. Yes, die. Go. Scatter. We can make some more money that way. But people still lived. Why? It was just like Priest Jackson asked, Why did Noah save all those animals, when all they're going to do is gnash? Why did Noah save his sons and his wife? Why'd he save himself?

Whenever Preacher saw Gene's Towing Service, Gene would pull out his new green bandana and wave it. Preacher would pet Pup and wave back.

Like all wrecker services, Gene's Towing carried a pistol. Preacher didn't know that, or he would have warned him about the rifle over the mantel. One early morning when the moon hadn't quite managed to set and the sun was just shaking his head, urging her downward with a polite chuckle, Gene's Towing Service was called to tow away a bright yellow pick-up that some drunk had left parked nearly against the Dairy Queen's front door. 'I'll do it cheaper if you give me a vanilla ice cream cone,' Gene's Towing Service had joked on the phone. 'I'll give you an extra large vanilla milkshake if you get the idiot's truck out from my front door. I can't even open it. It's Saturday, my busiest day, and customers won't be able to get in.' So Gene's Towing Service showed up and loaded the yellow pick-up onto his bed. Gene was licking a vanilla ice cream cone and laughing with the Dairy Queen owner when a drunken cattle farmer arrived. He got out of the car his wife was driving and stumbled toward the two men who were laughing. 'That's my truck,' he said, swaying forward. 'Why'd you park it in front of my door?' the Dairy Queen owner asked. 'Why wasn't you open when I wanted a burger and some fries?' the cattle farmer countered.

PREACHER:

So me and Pup got up early one Saturday. 'It's a good day for a ride, Pup,' I said. 'Let's fill up with some hamburgers and hot dogs and ice cream at the Dairy Queen.' Pup, she wagged her tail like always. (*Preacher now looks around, then under the picnic table, then speaks to a nearby girl in the crowd. The girl has two wild pigtails sticking from either side of her head.*) Did you see her? I wonder where she got off to now? (*The girl shakes her head, and Preacher looks up, resuming.*) I listened to the lady vet, you know, but not soon enough. Some scamp of a male wandered by and got Pup pregnant. She had three puppies on her first and only litter. The boy who wanted to make boxes for coffins took one. Todd and Elsa took the other two. I thought they might name them after their drowned son and that girl, but they didn't. Pup and me missed the puppies for a bit, and then we didn't.

Anyway, it was Saturday, and me and Pup drove to the Dairy Queen.

From about thirty yards away, I saw Gene licking a vanilla ice cream cone and laughing with the Dairy Queen guy. From Highway 28's other direction a blue car pulled into the lot and a man in a flappy red shirt jumped out from the passenger side and ran up to Gene and the Dairy Queen guy. The flappy red shirt started waving his hands and screaming. Me and Pup parked in the lot as Gene went to his truck and pulled out a long revolver. I powered down my windows on both sides of the truck. 'Don't,' I said. *Don't*, I thought. Pup gave a low whimper, just like she was also thinking, *Don't*. But Gene tucked the revolver into the back of his pants. He saw me and Pup and gave a wave. *Where's your new green bandana?* I thought. *Wave it instead. Wave it instead.* He walked back to where the man in the flappy red shirt was still yelling but was now trying to climb into his truck that sat chained on the bed of Gene's Towing Service's truck. A half-pint bottle fell from under the flappy red shirt. The man in the flappy red shirt cursed. Gene's Towing Service cursed and tugged at the man's pants leg to get him off the truck. The Dairy Queen owner got out his cell phone and punched in a number. A car whizzed by, tooting its horn happily. Pup growled. I thought, *Don't*. 'God damn it!' Gene's Towing Service yelled when the man kicked him. I thought of Father Jackson's list. I thought, *He already has. Damning it is what He excels at.* 'Fuck you and your front door! Fuck you and your towing service and your hundred twenty-six dollar bill!' the man in the flappy red shirt yelled. Gene reached behind his back. *Don't*, I thought. The man in the red shirt reached into his right pocket and pulled out a pistol. *Pop! Pop!* it went. Gene's Towing Service fell, his long silver revolver clattering on the blacktop. The woman sitting in the blue car screamed. A siren sounded.

MAN IN CROWD:

Jesus keeps a list all right. It's to mark the blessed from the damned.

WOMAN IN CROWD:

It's to remind us to obey him.

ANOTHER WOMAN IN CROWD:

It's to remind us to love one another, not shoot one another.

WOMAN IN CROWD:

It's to remind us that those who side with Satan will suffer eternal hellfire and bursting skin and bleeding ulcers and parched, dried mouths. Their fingertips will burst and bleed and itch and purge them forever. That's to remind them of the sins those foul fingers committed.

WOMAN IN CROWD:

Their minds too. Their minds committed sins, so their brains get crawly with beetles, and worms creep out their ears, which burn and then get better to heal and then burn even more. Even more, each time, for eternity. Even more. It's what they deserve.

MAN IN CROWD:

They burn to remind us not to be unnatural. They burn because our tongues must speak out against evil people when we hear them.

PREACHER:

Pup? Where are you, Pup? (*Pup scrambles up atop the table. She has a bright green tennis ball in her mouth. Her tail wags and she paws Preacher's leg.*)

. . . Preacher went to Gene's Towing Service's funeral. He never knew that Gene had a wife and two daughters, both of them in high school. *Pit bulls. We won't let go.* Gene's two daughters had not been enrolled in that school when the boy did the shooting. They were still in grade school then. Now they were pretty and all smart. Gene was just teaching them to drive, Preacher learned at the funeral. The boy at the boxing plant who'd died in the car wreck was their first cousin, Preacher learned. They'd taken his dog in when he died. *Small world*, Preacher thought. After the funeral he drove home and told Pup about it, that her puppy had a good home with two smart, pretty girls. Pup wagged her tail. Preacher gave her part of his hamburger and fries. He didn't tell her about Gene's Towing Service. But then she'd seen it, so she knew.

MATH SPEAKS: GO. SCATTER.

PREACHER:

I thought about lists. I thought of the many ways I could list them. Alphabetical, last name. Alphabetical, first name. Alphabetical, middle name. Alphabetical, nickname. I could list them by dates of death, or dates of birth. I could list them by their eye colors or their hair colors. I could list them by their height. Gene's Towing Service would be the tallest. The boxing plant boy would maybe be the shortest. I never knew any midgets. Maybe they aren't allowed in the county or even the state. I could list them by their skin: pale pink, white, yellow, tan, brown, black, purple-black. I could list them by their occupations at the time of their deaths: truck driver, student, housewife, clerk, waitress, factory worker, cop, priest, drug dealer.

   I wondered why I thought that last. The yellow-light shack was still on my mind. I drove by it on the way to Gene's Towing Service's funeral. I drove by it on the way back. I drove by it that evening with Pup. We slowed and looked. The yellow light was on, but it wasn't blinking. We drove over the railroad tracks. I thought of The Fairy Girl. How had I forgotten her on the list? What would be her occupation? Wanderer? Dreamer? Waif? *Human*, I decided. *Human*. It's occupation hard enough. Pup and me turned around and drove back. The yellow light was off.

. . . Was there a lull in the list? Two weeks? Three? Had the pen's ink dried? Maybe the printer had run out of paper? Or what if there really was a fresh new blueprint?

Preacher knew that even if he had walked over to Gene's Towing Service's truck at the Dairy Queen as the police and the ambulance came, even if he'd plucked up the lucky green bandana that had fallen from Gene's pocket onto the seat of the cab—well, his own luck still wouldn't change. Still, Gene should have been more careful about his good luck bandana. And Gene should have remembered that rule about mantels and guns.

Preacher and Pup drove around in the cooling fall weather. They looked in amazement at the colorful leaves. They pretended that those leaves were backstroking down to the ground, not falling. They pretended that they, too, were backstroking down to the ground, not falling.

There was one woman in the county who'd known Preacher's mother. Nancy Thompson was this woman's name. She'd actually met his mother before they moved into town. She was a nurse too, and had worked with his mother for eight years in some city. Preacher and Pup would stop by every week or so, bring Nancy Thompson three bakery cupcakes. She loved the bakery's cupcakes. Vanilla, that was what she loved. Pup did too. Pup couldn't eat chocolate, the lady vet with her starey eyes said.

NANCY THOMPSON:

You're so sweet to bring these by. *(She looks at Pup and bends to give her a pat.)* And I suppose you want one, as usual, don't you Pup? *(To Preacher.)* She's not a puppy now.

It would have been better if you'd named her 'New York Minute.'

PREACHER:

No, that would be too scary. It would be tempting fate even more than—

NANCY THOMPSON:

Did you know that your mother was in a hospital tent that got shelled? She was the only one who survived. Five doctors, four other nurses, sixteen soldiers—all killed.

PREACHER:

She never told me that.

NANCY THOMPSON:

You don't want to tell your children terrible things. There's terrible things enough waiting for them out there.

PREACHER:

I'm making a list.

NANCY THOMPSON:

Lists are false. Lists are terrible things.

... Preacher agreed. Then Nancy Thompson asked Preacher if he knew how his parents met. 'A sniper,' he said, 'got them together.' 'Yes, isn't it romantic? They were at a bar up in Cincinnati, Ohio. Your father started flirting with your mother. They learned they were in the war. They learned they were in the same area at the same time. They learned they were at the beach when that sniper killed a soldier. Your mother had a knife the sniper was carrying because some soldier who climbed up and found the sniper after they shot him, that soldier gave it to her, trying to charm her. As if a knife from a dead man would charm anyone.'

Preacher looked at the cupcake that was left. He realized the clerk at the bakery had given him a chocolate one. He went in there twelve, fifteen times a year for five years and ordered vanilla but she gave him a chocolate one.

NANCY THOMPSON:

Your mother told me she was pregnant when they married. The baby was a blue baby. It was stillborn, the umbilical cord wrapped around its neck. Doctors and technology weren't so swift in those days. So there. You had a sister, a baby sister.

PREACHER:

I didn't know that.

NANCY THOMPSON:

There's lots of things people don't know. That's a chocolate cupcake. I love chocolate.

MATH SPEAKS: GO. SCATTER.

PREACHER:

I thought you liked vanilla.

NANCY THOMPSON:

I do, but I love chocolate even better.

PREACHER: (*Looking out at the crowd, then under the picnic table.*) Has anyone seen Pup? She saved that woman's life that day.

MAN IN CROWD:

Didn't do much good, since she died the next morning.

WOMAN IN CROWD:

I heard that DHR investigated because she had broken ribs. I heard they thought maybe you were abusing her so you'd get her money.

MAN IN CROWD:

Miss Nancy didn't have any money except her social and a tiny bit of retirement.

WOMAN IN CROWD:

He up there didn't know that. Look at his eyes, how they cut from you.

ANOTHER WOMAN IN CROWD:

It's a shame, Miss Thompson treated him like a son. And all he could do was bring her the wrong cupcakes once every week or so.

LIZZIE, GIRL POET IN CROWD:

I know that I don't know.
A wise man said that once.
The things he thought he knew, he'd show.
The things he didn't, hung off, grapes in a bunch.

MOTHER IN CROWD:

I don't know why she's so sad all the time. Her sister and her brother, me and her daddy, we're happy-go-lucky.

WOMAN IN CROWD:

There's something different about her, all right.

MOTHER IN CROWD:

Her daddy thinks she's got poetic—

WOMAN IN CROWD:

Don't matter what he thinks about her so-called 'poetic genius.' There's something off and different about her. Just like that one up there on the picnic table, spouting his lies and stories.

MATH SPEAKS: GO. SCATTER.

ANOTHER WOMAN IN CROWD:

Puppy-stealer.

PREACHER:

The bakery opens early, 6 a.m. I stopped by the next day after graveyard shift work and bought three cupcakes, two chocolate for Ms. Thompson, one vanilla for Pup. All that time, I didn't know. About the chocolate, I mean. Ms. Thompson was right about all the things we don't know. We move as dumb and steady as the sun and moon. Maybe even dumber because we think we know. The moon and the sun, do those two talk and whisper to one another? We don't know. Do they know?

So me and Pup drove to Ms. Thompson's. We drove there to check on her because the day before when Ms. Thompson sent me to a closet in one of her rooms to fetch a blue box of photographs, she started choking on the cupcake I brought her. I was in another part of the house in a closet and didn't hear her choking. She'd sent me to the wrong room and the wrong closet anyway. But Pup, she came running in and barking at me. '*Bark! Bark! . . . Bark! Bark! Bark!*' She was so frantic that I went out, out from the room into the kitchen. Ms. Thompson was leaned back in the chair, clutching her throat. I got her up and did what the EMT classes said I should do. The piece of cupcake flew from her mouth onto the table. She finally caught her breath. 'You saved my life,' she said. 'Pup did,' I answered.

I told her that I hadn't heard her because I was back in that room, in the closet.

MS. THOMPSON:

Oh my. I sent you to the wrong room. That's not where those photos are. They're in the closet in my bedroom. (*She laughs, choking briefly, and laughing at that.*) Maybe I was being coy about sending a handsome man to my bedroom, do you think? But go on and fetch them. Pup will watch over me. First door on your left.

. . . Preacher found the blue box and brought it back. Ms. Thompson's thin, blue fingers skittered through the blue box and pulled out a photo. It was of a woman in uniform. She was looking up in the air, as if the photographer had hung a bunch of grapes almost near enough for her to reach. Almost. She had black, black, black hair. She was beautiful. She had a small smile, as if she knew those grapes were a trick and that she'd never get to taste them, so she wouldn't even try, though the photographer and his assistant kept talking about how juicy and sweet they were, and how if she just smiled enough, she'd get some.

MS. THOMPSON:

That's your mother, just before she went to the war. She told me that her smile disappeared permanent after the war. She told me that after the war she dreamed lists of dead G. I.'s at night. She told me she never saw their faces, but only their dog tags. She told me she heard those dog tags clink, one on top of the other, as someone dropped them into a box. She told me that occasionally in those dreams she thought she saw the hand that was dropping the tags, but she could never be certain, that maybe the hand was gloved, as if it didn't want to touch the unclean tags. Your daddy, he came over right before the end of the war. He was in only one fight, but it was enough, your mother told me. He lost two new friends he'd made. She thinks that maybe she'd been in the operation tent when one of them died, though she never told your daddy that. There's some things you just keep locked in your heart. You've got your momma's black hair.

PREACHER: *(Looking out at the crowd, who for once seem to be listening.)*

We all, I suppose, keep things locked that way. Maybe of night we tiptoe out of our bodies, leaving them lying warm and curled on our beds, and we spirit walk out to our yard and put our spirit hands on the rusty wheelbarrow out there and we spew all the nasty things from the day, from the week, from the month, spew them out of our spirit mouths like pieces of cupcake that have been choking us and we fill the wheelbarrow up with them and we tote them out to the highway, where we dump them, hoping some eighteen-wheeler will roar by and flatten them so they can sail away in the night breeze before morning comes.

LIZZIE, GIRL POET IN CROWD:

Our troubles keep close, so hard, so hard.
Then both troubles and we move on, move on.
The rocks and mountains, they watch from afar.
Come one longsome day, even they go gone.

PREACHER:

That young girl's right. We should all listen when she talks. (*He looks around.*) Pup? Pup, where are you? (*Looking at crowd, searching, then spotting one balding man with a sunburnt scalp.*) You. You're the one who shouted that it didn't do much good for me to save Ms. Thompson, since she died the next morning. Well, I guess you're right, just like that young girl's right about her poetry. Hey, has anyone seen Pup? She's getting old. She's got cataracts and can't see too well. I worry. She can still smell though. She can still hear and wag her tail in a slow thump. (*He looks at the crowd.*) I suppose the time has arrived. I suppose it's time to tell you about the shack and the blinking yellow S. O. S. light.

Yellow Fever

. . . Preacher and Pup went to Ms. Thompson's funeral and then burial. Pup sat on the ground next to Preacher. Two people turned around and glared. *What? What?* Preacher wondered. *Are you thinking dogs can't be here because dogs aren't pure? Because they aren't good enough? Dogs are good enough. They die too, don't they? That's good enough for anything.*

Ms. Thompson was Catholic, so the burial was held behind the Catholic church in a tiny plot. The church had a new priest who no one liked because he was Irish and spoke thickly and drank a lot. He had replaced Father Jackson. Preacher heard that he even made jokes about Father Jackson out playing on a swing. In Ireland, this new priest said, where times were rough, folk appreciated life. In Ireland, he said, no one would throw his life away playing on a swing. In Ireland, in Ireland, in Ireland. He didn't know Ms. Thompson, except to see her. 'She was a fine woman,' he said. 'She gave her widow's mite.' Ms. Thompson wasn't a widow, Preacher thought. She'd never married. He and Pup shared a chocolate cupcake once a week after that. Neither of them gave a care what the vet with her starey eyes said about chocolate and dogs.

PREACHER:

Time is like a swing. And time might even be a widow for all I know. But then, who could be time's husband? No, I think not, not a widow. No, time must swing alone. And we are her bastard children and she cradles us in her lap until we tumble. (*Preacher looks expectantly at Lizzie, the Girl Poet. He waits, but she remains silent. He leans toward her and waits some more, but she won't even blink. He gives a long sigh and returns to speaking.*) So I went in to work and made boxes, Pup stayed home and watched the house and yard. The plant owner came to me one morning and said, 'You've been here a long time. You can move to day shift if you want.' 'No,' I told him, 'Graveyard shift suits me fine.' (*A woman in the crowd coughs loudly to cover a laugh. Another woman brays.*) It was every very early morning, really being late night before dawn, that I always drove back to get Pup, and then we drove back to pass the shack with the yellow light. Every very early evening we did the same. I wouldn't drive by without Pup, since she was my good luck, like Gene's dark green bandana.

There were plenty more to add to the list that I wasn't keeping, that I was keeping. A two-car wreck, a logging truck turned over, a heart-attacked man on a bike over here from somewhere in Georgia, making some point about touring the country for trees, ecology, and fresh air. Todd, my elderly friend from the boxing plant. His wife and two remaining boys didn't even cry at the funeral.

They three stood and shook hands in a long receiving line and didn't cry. One of the boys was married by then. That boy's wife was pregnant. I looked at her belly and thought how it was good, wasn't it, that Todd and Elsa would get their wish.

Then one pre-dawn morning after work me and Pup drove by the shack. I'd taken Pup to work that night shift, since she looked at me so sad-eyed when I was about to leave. It was plenty warm, so she'd be all right in the truck. She'd even be all right in the field next to the plant, because she was getting too old to run, so she'd just walk around sniffing in the field there, but mostly just lie in the cab of the truck, sometimes sticking her snout out the open window. Sniffing. So anyway, that morning in the quiet and in that darkest hour that was supposed to come just before dawn, we set out right away to drive by the shack.

I looked to Pup: 'You know what, Pup? I believe we missed a couple-three-four days somehow.' Pup cocked her head and whined.

The shack's yellow porch light was blinking like it had only that one time before. 'Someone needs us, Pup,' I said. Pup leaned and gave my pants leg a lick. There wasn't a car in the dirt driveway when I pulled in. I'd never seen a truck or car in that driveway, though the yellow porch light or some other house light was usually on.

There wasn't even any gravel in the drive, just dirt. I used my flashlight, but still I stumbled on a clod. And then I stumbled in a hole. A smell lay about the house—no, not cheese and gangrene; no, not the acrid stench of death. It was flowers. I remembered the flowery funeral of the man and boy, the man who didn't believe in doctors and hospitals and his boy, who I guessed maybe didn't believe in them either, and Anna, the wife and mother who thought I might be an angel come to save them. Would an angel prescribe blue and red pills? Would an angel use a laser wand for microsurgery? Would an angel? . . . The smell was flowers, all right. Just like the tiers and tiers of flowers at that dual funeral. But it was late spring, early summer, so flowers were good, not unnatural like in winter.

I stepped onto the porch, and just like last time my motion edged the door open. Maybe I was an angel and just didn't know it.

MAN IN CROWD:

Or maybe you're a devil and just don't know it.

WOMAN IN CROWD:

He knows it all right! And we know it too!

PREACHER:

I want to assure you that I did think that, I really did. That I was a devil, or at least that I was some type of dark servant. It gave me pause. But I had to go on. I had to go on in. At the door, the flower smell disappeared. Now the rot of death spilled. I shined my light on the same ratty brown couch in the front room. A limp plastic grocery bag sat there on it. I could see baby food jars in the sack. The card table was gone. There was a ratty red chair now in the middle of that room, not even against a wall like you'd think. All around the ratty red chair, stuffing was scattered on the bare wood floor. I gagged from the smell of the shack and swayed, but I shined my light on through into the kitchen. The wooden table was still there. A body was slumped over it. Its right arm hung down. It was a woman wearing a thin, pale yellow sundress, but the top of her skinny body glowed so white that it made the sundress look dirt brown. Her two feet were bare. They were dark, though, so maybe she had on socks. I walked over and touched her shoulder. It was cool, just like the night air around the house. No need to put my two fingers to her carotid, but I did anyway, like the EMT classes told me. You can never tell, the EMT class said, even though you always could.

Sunrise light began peeping in. There was another note by her left hand, tented to stand just like before. When I read it, I could see that it was written the same neat way. '*Save my baby.*' And beneath that, '*J.*' So Jolene, Janice, Jessica, Jenny, or Jennifer. Josephine. I thought I heard a baby cry. I rushed to the back door. It was only the merry-go-round clothesline in the wind. A storm was coming fast. The little sunrise light that had started peeping, it shut its eyes like it was saying goodbye. 'So long,' I told it. Then I shined my light back into the kitchen. A syringe lay on the table, the needle glistering and glittery in my flashlight's light. I hadn't noticed the syringe because of the note. '*Save *my baby.'* A baby somewhere? Where? A baby? I found a light switch and turned the kitchen lights on. Blood had puddled, drying on the floor by the woman's left leg. Something had been eating at above her ankle, a rat maybe, because tiny, dried blood splotches led away. Maybe from the same animal that had torn out the stuffing in the red chair in the middle of the floor in the front room. I could see that she didn't have on socks, that her feet were dark blue because the blood had settled in them. A baby somewhere? Where? A baby? Where? To my right, the iron door to the potbelly stove was half-open. I hurried. I bent. I shined my light in toward movement. Maggots, hundreds of maggots on what looked like a newborn, lying on a pink shirt. I closed my eyes, but still saw the squirming. *No! Not maggots! No! That baby is still alive! It is still breathing and squirming and moving! That's what I see!*

    I couldn't fit both arms in, so I tugged at the pale yellow cotton shirt, careful not to drop the baby or have it twist and fall on the floor. You're supposed to support newborns by their head. Their heads and necks are sensitive, not yet formed. Even their skullcap is not yet formed. I learned that in EMT classes. I carefully tugged the cotton shirt that the newborn was wrapped in. I tugged it free of the potbelly stove and looked down. No, no. Yes, yes, yes. Hundreds of squirming maggots. I dropped the baby and the shirt, and even more maggots squirmed out, spilling onto the floor. Maybe a thousand. I gagged.

WOMAN AT TABLE:

My baby. Is my baby all right?

PREACHER:

I—

WOMAN AT TABLE:

I knew someone would come in time to save my baby. I left baby food on the couch. Peas. Carrots. Carrots are good for their eyes. I stole the jars from Wal-Mart. They have those cameras, but I know how to trick them. I knew someone would come. I put it in the stove because that's off the floor and made of iron. Iron is safe. Iron is good. Quick, go get the peas. I think the baby's a girl. I don't know who the father is. Peas are good for girls.

PREACHER: (*Turning to look at the dead woman at the table.*)

Yes, I've heard that, too. What's your name?

WOMAN AT TABLE:

Cecilia. I'm Father Jackson's sister. When I heard he had a church here, I came. But he never found me.

PREACHER:

He died.

WOMAN AT TABLE:

Died.

PREACHER:

Yes, he died.

WOMAN AT TABLE:

Say there, where's your doggie? I always give your doggie a doggie biscuit and you always get a little leprechaun. You always look like you need some luck, you know, that's why I wish you a leprechaun. My little baby's a real bundle of luck. I want to name him Patrick. You'll be needing to feed him some of that baby food I left. If only I . . . if . . . I only . . . I should never have listened.

PREACHER:

Listened?

WOMAN AT TABLE:

Don't listen to her! That's my baby. That's the baby I was carrying at the lake when those water moccasins fanged my boyfriend and me! It's my baby! Are you going to save my baby? I put it in the iron stove to keep it safe. You're a certified EMT, aren't you? But that didn't do us much good at that lake when all you did was run around the shore and drop your cell phone and scream a lot. Snakes can't hear, you know.

PREACHER:

I never learned to swim. I'm afraid of water.

WOMAN AT TABLE:

Water? What's water got to do with the with of what? Oh yeah, now I remember. Weren't we going to take swimming lessons over in the city right before my dad got that job and that transfer? It's my baby over there in that stove. I put it there—I think he's a boy—I put it there to keep it safe. It's iron you know.

PREACHER:

Sharon?

WOMAN AT TABLE:

Of course it's me. And that's *your* baby, too, lying in that wood stove. You need to get him out right now and feed him. There's some peas out there on the couch. I heard that peas are good for boys.

PREACHER:

I've heard that, too. How can I be the father? We were just turning fifteen when you moved away.

WOMAN AT TABLE:

Mary was a lot younger than fifteen. And maybe Joseph too. Read your Bible.

PREACHER:

But all we ever did was kiss and hug a lot. We were scared.

WOMAN AT TABLE:

Lois and your friend Jimmy told us how to do it. Don't you remember? As if anyone needs instructions. Men and women, they have these feelings.

PREACHER:

But we just kissed—

WOMAN AT TABLE:

Kissed? Are you some type of hemophilia cadaver pervert? We never kissed. You opened my stone dead hand and a lightning bug flew out. I'm sure the bug thanks you, even if I don't. I left my baby ten miles back on those tracks, by a grocery store where I knew someone would find it. Maybe they did and then put it in that stove, I don't know. I asked you to stay by me so that dogs or coyotes or possums wouldn't eat at me, so I do guess I need to thank you for that. So there, so now. Thanks. Thanks for that.

WOMAN AT TABLE:

Don't listen to her. I have a poem for you.

PREACHER:

Lizzie?

WOMAN AT TABLE:

Did you think my name was Eve? Did you think your name was Adam?

LIZZIE, GIRL POET IN CROWD:

The fires in our heads do thunder and roar.
The fires in our hearts do sear and soar.
Poor humans, poor creatures!
Newborn, only to stumble, drop dead on a floor.

WOMAN IN CROWD: (*Picking up a stone and throwing it at Lizzie.*)

I hate you! We all hate you! (*Turning to Preacher.*) I hate you too! We all hate you!

PREACHER: (*Ignoring the woman and scrambling off the picnic table and raising his right arm to point at a dog with a bright hunter-green tennis ball in its jaws. The dog wags its tail and runs toward Preacher.*) Pup! Where on earth have you been? I've been asking these fine people about you. I worried that you were . . .

. . . Pup stumbles on the ground, for her front right paw is turning into dust that trails behind in the air as she runs. Preacher's right arm drops. Then it turns to dust, which slithers toward his shoulder in waves, like a snake swallowing a rat, like a fire consuming autumn leaves, until only dirty gray-white dust remains to ease to the ground in what may appear to be a backstroke but is not, for the gray-white dust drops slowly in a fine powder, half supported through the air, half swirling through the air, all the while inexorably longing for the patient dirt below. This movement resembles two long-separated lovers, unbelieving their luck and walking toward one another, say at a train station, say on a crowded New York City sidewalk, say at a bus station, say at an airport, say in a bar after a war, their arms opening wider, their steps coming faster, turning to a trot, a run, a hard sprint. *New York minute, New York minute*, bids a hidden loudspeaker system. A breeze lifts and the entire crowd begins to swirl, spiraling upward in a bone-white dust cloud toward the sun. Or is it toward the moon? There may be a residual sifting sound, there may be only silence. Pup has disappeared, though the green tennis ball rolls forward by momentum. It bumps over a pebble or possibly a crack, but keeps its course, like a fabled perpetual motion machine. For how long? *Go, scatter*. Preacher has disappeared, though his two leather boots face forward. They remain that way without him, splayed open as if welcoming the rolling hunter-green tennis ball. The ball affords the only movement on the ground. Everything else swirls toward the sun. *Go. Scatter.* There may be a sifting sound, there may be only silence. On this day, the moon just happens to be glowing—beautiful, pale, and nervous like a daytime moon will be. Look, though, look! If you were there and you looked up at her, you'd swear she was smiling, just as if she'd won some grand bet. Listen, though, listen! If you were there, you might hear a sifting sound, but it would not be the moon making it. You might—yes, you might!—hear only silence.

LIZZIE, GIRL POET IN CROWD: (*Speaking even as she crumbles into gray-white dust.*)

Ring around the rosy,
Pocket full of posies.
Scream, scream, but don't make a sound.
Listen, listen, we all fall down.

MOON:

I won the bet.

SUN:

No, I did.

They both laugh and begin a tango. Or is it a waltz?

ALSO BY JOE TAYLOR

STORIES

Ghostly Demarcations
The World's Thinnest Fat Man
Some Heroes, Some Heroines, Some Others
Masques for the Fields of Time

NOVELS

Bad Form
Back to the Wine Jug
The Theoretics of Love
Pineapple: A Comic Novel in Verse
The Alleged Woman
Oldcat & Ms. Puss: A Book of Days for You and Me
Let There Be Lite: How I Came to Know and Love Gödel's Incompleteness Theorem

Printed in the USA
CPSIA information can be obtained
at www.ICGtesting.com
LVHW040018260124
768987LV00003B/32